KING

OF

THE O'MALLEYS

DOUG McPHILLIPS

Also by Doug McPhillips:

Other Visionary Stories:
NOVELS.

From Darkness to Light.
Awake to my Gutted Dream.
The Sword of Discernment.
Santiago Traveller.
I'Prophet.
Masters at my table.
The Guru of Jerusalem.
We is me Upside Down. (Autobiography)
The Wicklow Way.
The Adventures of Ace McDice,
Stretch Deed & Moonshine Melody.
Instant Karma & Grace.
The Credo.
Reflections of an Old Man.
A Camino Guide Book.
Country Camino. (Album)
Santiago Traveller. (Album)

Doug McPhillips April 2023

ISBN. 978-0-6454421-8-4

National library of Australia Catalogue-in publication data:
Holy Bible, New International Version, Hodder & Stoughton 1984.
Alcoholics Anonymous: AA World Service, 4th Edition 2001.
Hoyle A. R. King O'Malley. Globe Press 1981. Google research- Authors Unknown.A booklet published and distributed by King O'Malley titled, 'The Commonwealth Bank - The Facts of its Creation'. Reserve Bank of Australia Archives, 18/7329.

This book is a work of both fact and fiction. Where poetic licence is used to turn fact into fiction, names have been changed to protect the innocent.

To the memory of Pop and Nana,
my Irish grandparents,
and for kinfolk who still enjoy the craic.

Forward:

King O'Malley is best remembered as a colourful and at times controversial politician in the period following Australia's federation. He was
a significant figure in the initiative to create a national bank with central
banking responsibilities. Ambiguity surrounds the formative years of
King O'Malley's early life. By his own account, he was born in Quebec,
Canada, but other sources suggest he began life in Kansas, United
States. Following the death of his father in the Civil War, O'Malley was
sent to live with his aunt and uncle in New York. He received a very
limited education and spent much of his time working at his uncle's
small bank from the ages of 14 to 22.

From the age of 22, O'Malley pursued a career as an insurance salesman and real estate agent on the United States' west coast. He migrated
to Australia in 1888 – living at first in Melbourne, before Hobart and
Zeehan in Tasmania, Coolgardie in Western Australia and Adelaide.
O'Malley claimed to have arrived in Australia in Port Alma, Queensland, before journeying on foot to Sydney, then Melbourne and Adelaide – however, historians have regarded the tale of this dramatic arrival as dubious.

This King of the O'Malley's is still our most legendary figure of Australian Parliamentary history- a man of eccentric behaviour, but with the
will and strength of character to become the longest serving member of
parliament of the original characters who established our Australian
parliament at the inaugural federal election in 1901. He honed his
rhetorical style of persuasion serving for a single term in the South Australian House of Assembly then served in the House of representatives
from 1901-1917 as a foundation member of the Australian labor party.
O'Malleys grandiosity and Irish-American charm into the South Australian Parliament (1896-1899) saw him wielded his campaigns for
lavatories in railway carriages, seats for female shop assistance and
the Married Women's Protection League which all won him great notoriety.

King O' Malley is best remembered for his role serving two terms as
Minister for Home Affairs (1910-1913; 1915-1916), and his key role in
the development of Canberra as well as his advocacy in the establishment of a national Commonwealth Bank, as well as the construction of
the Trans-Australian Railway. Whilst his political career, aided by his

style of 'spread-eagle' rhetoric, carried him into the Federal sphere and continued his characteristic wild proposals, strong reformist policies and fervent industry reforms, his clashes with colleagues and the public service always kept him in the limelight of voters.

This account of O' Malley's life comes from his own lips and what has been written about him recorded from the newspapers of his times, and the word of mouth accounts of others who have no doubt embellished tales of him as much as he did of himself.

So, in this little story, I being of Irish decent myself use my own narratives, broadly speaking, in a way of linking factual events, mythic narratives of events that grant them not simply meaning but a kind of importance in the life of this larger than life character. It is for you the reader to discern fact from fiction in this account of a man of significance. So to begin....

Contents.

King O'Malley

'Battle hard, never give up
a good cause, never drink
stagger juice, smoke, or lose
your sense of humour.'

King O'Malley, 1952

INTRODUCTION.

At the local School of Arts in the township of my childhood an event took place which still stands-out in my memory as a momentous occasion. It was a celebration of the athletic feats of Marjorie Jackson, who became known as the 'Lithgow Flash.' Jackson was born in Coffs Harbour, NSW in 1931 which may explain why she visited North Coast townships to tell her story to schoolchildren. She was raised in Lithgow, NSW where she trained under car headlights in winter. In 1949 she stunned the athletic world by beating Dutch Olympic champion Fanny Blankers-Koen in Sydney. In January 1950 she set the first of her 10 world records by running 10.8 secs for 100 yards (91.44 metres) in Adelaide. Marjorie was also a member of three world record-breaking relay teams.

At the 1950 Auckland Commonwealth Games Marjorie won four gold medals with the sprint double and two medley relays. Marjorie made her real mark however at the 1952 Helsinki Olympics where she won both the 100 and 200 metres. The 100 yards (91.44 metres) was in a world record 11.5 secs and her winning margin of nearly four metres is the greatest winning margin in Olympic women's history. She set a world record in both her heat and semi-final of the 200 metres (23.4) before winning the final comfortably. She was the first Australian woman to win Olympic gold for track and field. After Helsinki, Marjorie went to Gifu, Japan where she set a world record of 11.4secs.

This story is not about her, nor her list of successes as an athlete, rather the year of her visit when she told of how to be a champion athlete. The year stands in my memory for it was early in 1953, as far as I recall, when she made that visit and speech to us schoolchildren assembled in the old School of Arts. For it was in that old timber building, which was soon to be torn down in the interest of progress, that two other events occurred that year. I was near nine year of age at the time, so childhood memories are full of imagination and like the tale that follows may include some make believe. It was a busy year for events on that stage. Soon after the 'Lithgow Flash' told her story, the 'Slim Dusty Show' was staged and I remember Gordon Parsons, a local musician and poet sang some songs backing Slim on that stage. He was there with the comical character of Chad Morgan, the 'Sheik from Scrubby Creek' as he was known. Of course, this was well before Gordon penned the song ' The Pub with no Beer,' and sold it to Slim for five quid in the local pub of the same name at Taylor's Arm. Slim went on to sell over one million copies of that hit he recorded it in 1957.

So, if memory serves me correctly, 1953 was the   year the first Macksville Gift Athletic Carnival was held- an event that is still runs today, a stones throw from where the Old School of Arts once stood. It was also the year that Ashton's Circus and Zoo arrived and paraded through the streets of our township promoting the Circus event one summer evening. Well that was well after the 'Lithgow Flash' and Slim Dusty had hit the road again.

 No, the event that sticks in my mind the most is the story that follows. It was a play in late October 1953 in that old timber building   the 'School of Arts' that captured the imagination of that small boy. It was not the play story of King O' Malley which later fired my imagination, but that of C.K. Dennis "Sentimental Bloke." Bill is a low life Wool-loomooloo larrikin, who vows to abandon his life of gambling (playing Two-up) and drinking after a spell in gaol following a raid on a two up game. He falls in love with Doreen, who works in a pickle factory, but faces competition from a more sophisticated rival, Stror 'at Coot. Crucial to the success of The Sentimental Bloke was the fact that it was a masculine romance. It was a love story expressing heterosexual romantic feeling from a male point of view and in a self-consciously masculine way. As such it touched a cultural nerve. The war and early inter-war years were rife with confusion about men's relationship to women and romance. Australian men had been expected to be warriors during the war, but upon return were expected to transform into caring spouses.

The Bloke helped audiences to navigate these conflicting messages. Though written in verse, the narrative was what we might now call a romantic comedy. Its humour sprang from the fact that Bill was the antithesis of a romantic type, yet he proved himself a hopeless romantic just the same. In the parlance of the day, Bill was an Australian "larrikin." It insisted that it was possible for a modern Australian man to be romantic without compromising his masculinity, provided he did so in a sufficiently straightforward manner and steered clear of "Yankee" suavity.

The currency of The Sentimental Bloke (as it became known) grew rather than waned. It became a multi-media phenomenon, comprising a silent film and travelling stage musical, and it was frequently recited on radio and in concert halls. The idea of 'The Bloke' stuck with me like an itch I could not scratch. This was until a story more in keeping with the times came on the scene, but that was not until a couple of decades later when I was encouraged to play a part in a play loosely based on The Legend of King O' Malley- a 1970 musical written for stage by Bob Ellis and Michael Brody. The Sentimental Bloke was just a story but in the case of King O' Malley it was real life or was it?

Somehow "The Blokes" story and O' Malley's life seem to marry each other in humour and sentimentally. For in both instances they were romantics facing struggles with matters of the heart but for entirely different outcomes.' The rambunctious and unreliable musical odyssey through the life and times of 'American-born' King O'Malley, founding member of our House of Reps, father of our national capital and advocate for the creation of my tale, with a splash or two of Sentimental bloke tossed in for good measure was to be my template for writing this book. I did have a copy of Brody and Ellis play which I had borrowed from the library in my days of married bliss, but I returned it to the library with another book," King O' Malley: Man and Statesman, Author, Dorothy M. Catts. Publisher in 1957.

The memory of reading about O' Malley's life, the play I acted in and those book references were all I had to go on for the writing of this novel I had come to believe would transpire sooner rather than later. For I had attempted to borrow those books again but no trace of either book in library archives could be found. I was about to give up hope of finding a template to work from and was heading to University reference material when I happened upon a copy of A.R. Hoyle's "King O' Malley: 'The American Bounder', a 1981 version of his life. So armed with this book and an account of O' Malley's life from the museum of the Reserve Bank of Australia, and various past newspaper articles of his life story, I now had the template to unfold, with poetic licence, an account of 'The Kings' life be it real or imagined.

So dear reader, know that I have had this story embedded in my subconscious since childhood to some degree and I make no excuse for its fiction as the creative imagination does take precedence over the logical linear brain side in this story. To be fair, it has come from King O' Malley's version of events of his life more than my own interpretation.

CHAPTER 1.

AS KING SAW IT

In a little house in the Melbourne suburb of Albert Park an old man sat by a well stoked fire in a vacant and pensive mood. It was a cold and bleak mid-winter's day in 1950 and the occupant sat patiently by the fireplace awaiting special guests for a pre arranged lunch engagement. Although age 93 at the time, he was still actively engaged in his business affairs and the political goings on in both State and Federal politics despite having been retired from active politics since 1917. The old man in that small lounge room wall papered in a large pattern and decorated with volumes of Hansards and cartoons of himself was the infamous King O' Malley.

He had suffered much ill health in his midlife due to the enormity of his work load travelling the country as an insurance salesman, buying up old slum dwellings and renting them out to the poor and destitute for fair rental terms, often collecting the rent himself. Although he was to live another forty years, he was frequently ill and feeling sorry for himself and he probably would not have endured the strain of it all if it wasn't for his dutiful wife Amy who nurtured him like a child, listened to his ranting and ravings and stood by his side until the day he died. The little house in Albert park was not Amy's idea of a suitable house for a retired Commonwealth Minister, but her husband refused to consider moving to better living quarters for although he was rich and famous, his tastes were simple, and despite his wealth could not imagine why anyone would won't a more elaborate home.

Well before "The King of the O'Malley's" had entering politics, he gained much notoriety in making use of his knack of oratory and devil may care stunts. The flamboyant cheek of the man was built into his nature and served him well in his varied political career that has been written into Australian folk law. For he had much to tell in his dotage of his younger days on the frontiers of America and his life as the last surviving member of the first federal parliament and did much in his retirement defending his legacy. His political views combined with his personal background and personality traits made him a controversial figure during his career, and his life to this day has continued to attract public interest.

So a little about this man of dubious stories and flamboyancy, from the time of his arrival in Australia in 1888, before we venture back into that little lounge room. Prior to entering Federal politics the King of the O' Malley's cut his teeth in the political arena as a member of the South-Australian Parliament for Encounter Bay from 1896-1899, and then the Australia Parliament Member in Tasmania from 1901-1903, when during his term he had proclaimed himself the founder of the first national bank, the Commonwealth Bank, of which the amount of credit he deserves for its creation has often been debated both inside the political walls of parliament and in newspapers articles. King had served two terms in Federal parliament as a Labor Party member and under his guidance oversaw the construction of the Trans- Australian Railway, and the early development of the new national capital. He was also instrumental in the banning of alcohol sales in the Australian Capital Territory, a cause dear to his heart from his younger pioneering days in America, before his arrival 'Down Under', to use an American colloquialism.

So back to that little lounge room and the arrival of his guests. Whilst O' Malley would sometimes buy and cook fowl for special guests himself, on this occasion Amy had prepared a simple meal for lunch that day. King had recently purchased an ice cream machine and in keeping with his image as an American he took delight in serving his guests the desert. At the luncheon that day was James Catts, and his second wife Dorothy. James Catts had been a former unionist, politician and retired businessman, who during WW1 had been the director of voluntary recruitment in new South Wales and ran a weekly magazine "Call to Arms." The Catts were the closest friends, and they often stayed over when in Melbourne, as did the O' Malley's frequently stay at the Catt's house at Huntley's Point in Sydney. Others at that lunch were the Burley Griffins. Walter Burley Griffin, as a young Chicago American architect and landscape architect, had prepared the winning design for the building of the capital city of Canberra and to be sure he was always indebted to O'Malley for suggesting he should submit his ideas for consideration. Also present were John Arthur and his wife from Home Affairs. John was an Australian lawyer and politician. He was a member of the Australian Labor Party and like O' Malley were elected to federal parliament at the 1913 federal election, after a successful career at the

Victorian Bar. Also present was the former Governor-General, Lord Denman, which was possibly the reason for the lunch guests to be all together at the table on that day. Oh! and at one end of the table was an extra guest at O' Malley's invitation; Pat Williams, a journalist renowned for her timely stories of famous people in the press.

So we take up the story from Pat William's press article as she recounted the dinner conversation and recollections of those present at the O' Malley' for that lunch. "…he lives in a small suburban Melbourne cottage and to his recollection was the true founder of the Commonwealth Bank. O' Malley recounts that after the 1914 election, he was appointed 'Minister for External Communication' in the mammoth legal battle between the Australian trading banks and the Chifley Government has kept the status of the Commonwealth Bank and its functions before the nation as top political issues for nearly a year.So from behind the screen of a long retirement, the man who founded the "People's Bank" in other critical days has been watching the crisis that has come upon the great institution his vision created. King O'Malley, like the stormy petrels of the present political upheavals, was the product of an age of great change and, tough time's searchlight has inevitably swung wide of him, he has remained to observe and assess! 'The King" was a transgressor extraordinaire, and although the details of his rich story are all but forgotten by most, he remains peerless in our history as a combination of statesman and buffoon. He calls 92-year-old Bernard Shaw his junior (by a year) and he has lived in quiet retirement at his modest Bridport street, Albert Park cottage for just over 30 years. But there is still much about the rangy figure to recall the miffed, insolent Yankee who imported into the first Federal Parliament a pince-nez, Broadway showmanship, and a disregard for orthodoxy which kept the austere legislature quaking to its barely-set foundations.

Still an Orator, looking in on "the King" today, as I did, and find him entertaining old friends. O'Malley, the orator, it is soon clear, can still hold an audience. In response to his wit and shameless showmanship, no deference to his age is needed. Neither is the sting altogether gone from the verbal lashes so often felt by his political opponents. Wait for him to start talking, as inevitably he will, about "much of everything." See his eyes brighten. It is easy to sit back in the living room where the project was conceived and strategy planned and enjoy with him, the stew of the biggest of his many. King O'Malley recalls his entry into politics was an underling and had an eventful three-year term in the South Australian Legislative Assembly. He went on to the House of Representatives, first for Tasmania and later as a member for Darwin. He bounced and bothered Parliament until he was defeated in 1917 after differing from Prime Minister Hughes on conscription.

He had held the Home Affairs portfolio through two Fisher Ministries and in the first Hughes' Cabinet. He recalls that he peddled his bank scheme vainly among both political parties for 10 years before he realised that his open tactics were only building stronger opposition. So he went under-ground. Five months later, he used the famous "torpedo brigade" he had formed-a caucus within Caucus-to win his fight at the meeting of October 5, 1911. One of "the King's" men moved the motion to establish the bank, and it was adopted before Prime Minister Fisher could do more than rail against being beaten by "a Yankee bounder."

As he indulges his always uninhibited ego by surveying the present great prosperity of the bank, he mocks in Scotch tones the jeremiad of "Brother Fisher" that it would be closed in six months. His discourses on banking policies and lightning mental calculations in thousands and millions recall the financial wizardry which neither friend nor enemy could match. The main outlet for it today is in compiling his income-tax returns, whereon it is his habit to describe his occupation as "death dodger."

As a Father of Canberra, his Bank is the brightest, but not the only gem in "the King's" legislative crown as he is quick to remind you. It was he who moved the motion in the House which ultimately secured for the Commonwealth authorities 583,000 acres which Canberra can never be sold without an Act of Parliament, and he laid the foundation stone of-the Commencement Column in 1913. He claims credit, too, for London's Australia House and for preference to unionists. He was the first Minister in charge of construction of the transcontinental, railway. His joyful exclamation when he got the job was "My, what a lot of boodle!"

King O'Malley has only one interjector to admonish today-his Scottish-born wife, who is about 20 years his junior. And, for that a kindly comment suffices, "Tiow, Amy, don't run on sol." Her usual response is to run her hand fondly through his white mane. Often they have to tell each other not to get so excited about the bank, in his palmy days. The King" cracked his interjectors harder. When a newly-elected member referred to him as a "damned Yankee bounder" and called himself a self-made man, "the King" was quickly into the battle. "I ask the House to regard the honourable member who confesses he is a self made man and thereby relieves the Almighty of an awful responsibility," he came back. One of his most telling speeches was his shortest He was leaving a Tasmanian west coast port after his defeat and some electors came to the ship expecting to hear his swan song. All they heard as "the King" leaned over the rail was: "You convicts and sons of convicts, farewell!" A member of the press at 'the Kings' farewell to Tasmania asked about his national bank ideas :"But how will you run this bank? What is your banking system?" Mr.O'Malley had replied "Simplicity itself. You put your money in the slot we do the rest."

Mr. King O'Malley-The loss of that fight in him unwillingly put him into retirement, but "the King" had been winning and losing battles long before he came to Australia. His parents were Irish farmers; and he was born-in Canada just across the United States border from Vermont. " I only missed becoming President of the United States by yards," he to says. He left the farm in his early teens, moved on New York, after leaving college, began the workings of the outside world from the inside of a Broadway bank. The bank wasn't prepared to adopt the reforms, the youth proposed so vigorously, so he went west along with others in one of the most resplendent eras of American history. He started to sell books, but because "book larrikin '" wasn't much in demand in the Wild West he turned to land speculation, and sales alongside a railway line were poor so he erected great posters proclaiming:. "The World For Sale by King O' Malley." Then without drawing breath, still holding his lunch guests wide eyed attention, proclaimed religion and elected himself to the clergy and became a roving preacher hurriedly through the South. The last remark of his latter religious zeal and movement against the sale and drinking of alcoholic liquor which he called 'stagger juice' still raised laughs around that lunch table for his close friends."

According to King he contracted tuberculosis whilst on his rounds in fair weather and fowl and his weight fell to around seven stone. A doctor gave him six months to live and advised him to go too Queensland.

He took the doctor's advice and now he's a nonagenarian. Keeping healthy in the business of growing old, King O'Malley hasn't entirely conformed; He is as erect as a guardsman. His face, a healthy pink and white is unlined, and each morning he goes through a series bending, twisting and stretching exercises which would dismay many men half his age. He has his daily tipple in the Malley household from a jar winch contains the juice of five lemons and five oranges mixed with a gallon of water. The King still maintains Australia's future would be better if young would ' leave stagger juice alone' and put that money saved in the Commonwealth bank. Always a daily news reader, O'Malley eats the financial news with the business of the nation on his mind. His parting words to me were *"continue to study banking me ole, for it is the science of life and people don't know it!"*

Of course this newspaper account of what O' Malley had related at that dinner table may well be factual but his former account of his life is subject to conjecture, in the light of O'Malley's historic accounts of changing his story of his lifetime on the American frontier in the hay days of following the slogan: "Go west young man." Least of all his account of the circumstance that he related about his arrival on Australian shores. For it varied considerably from what can now be gleaned as maybe a more factual account than O' Malley's colourful story and the circumstances surrounding his arrival.

The truth of his story pre and post his arriving in Australia varied many times in accord with his mood and recall of the imagination of a true raconteur who could pull an audience, gauge by the mood of the attendance who wanted to know more about him. Much more so the account of the origin of his birth and upbringing. O' Malley's versions of the time and place of his birth depend on the importance of the location in as much as it later related to his proof of being a British subject to lawfully justify his presence as an Australian politician. His time and place of birth was always a subject of unproven mystery as equally was his account of his latter days in the wild west of the Americas in the second half of the nineteenth century prior to his arrival here late 1887 or early 1888. It is still unproven if O' Malley was actually an American citizen, in which case he would not have been accepted as a British subject and would not have been able to stand for a seat in State or Federal parliament. However, "the King' was not going to let such a thing block then opportunities that he envisaged for his -place in Australian's foundations.

So his story varied according to circumstances as it did in all things of this bounder. So it was that O' Malley justified his citizenship as a British subject knowing that no the records of birth could be found in either Canadian nor America, for both the frontier land kept know no records of birth at the time. According to O' Malley he was conceived in July 1854 at Valley Field in the North of New England. His mother Ellen O' Malley, faced with the imminent birth of her first child was alone, as her husband was far away with his regiment on the Oregon Trail and couldn't be reached to let him know of her immediate circumstance. It had been her husband William O' Malley's wish that the child be born in the United States, but although she wished to obey him, her need for family and friends was greater, so she suddenly made up her mind to hurriedly cross the unmarked Canadian boarder to be with her sister Maryanne and her husband, a young English doctor. There at Stanford Fram, on July 4th she gave birth to a son who was christened King, after her maiden surname. So as he professed by chance and a distance of a few hundred yards, King O' Malley was deprived of the opportunity to become President of the United States.

This was the story which O' Malley told in his later years when questioned of his birth assumed importance. Like so many stories of O' Malley's life, this story appears to do more credit to his political acumen and his imagination than his ability to tell the truth, the whole truth and nothing but the truth. Through the eons of time now there can be no certainty of the truth of the event of his Canadian citizenship, that he was actually born on the 4th of July 1854, that his father was actually a soldier whom he later claimed was killed in the Civil War or that his mothers maiden name was Ellen King.

Whilst for most of mankind the place of birth is of little importance in King O' Malley's case it was ultimately based upon the ultimate importance of his legal right to his Australian political career and the numerous opponents and enemies who believed, but could not prove that he was not a British subject, but rather an American alien, for neither his marriage certificate nor his death certificate give an actual date nor place of birth. When he was making his first entry into parliament an inspired biography in the"Adelaide Advertiser " at the time he gave his birth to be 2nd July and only later did change his birth date to be July 4th in an apparent acknowledgement fo his American origin. Mysteriously, as early as 1896, O' Malley is on record as advancing his age to a birth year of 1858 and he maintained that until 1940. He being one of the very few surviving members of the first Federal parliament probably felt that it added to his dignity to add four years to his actual age of eighty-two.

More important to him were the facts of his place of birth and his parentage. If he was an American citizen, then he sat for over twenty years in the Australian parliament illegally. On the other hand, if his version of his birth is true, then he was hounded unfairly for decades by his numerous enemies. Of course, when he arrived on our shores in the 1880s the tall tawny, good looking man, flamboyantly dressed, who spoke with an American accent, had declared himself American at the time, and was forever praising the United States and all things American. In a letter to the editor of a newspaper, not long after his arrival, he declared himself to be: "…a humble sovereign citizen of the supreme nation, the United States." He had at the time entered into a contract as a salesman of Life Insurance, and wished to portray an kind of reputable style as a stance by easily publicity with his clothing, accent and easy going American geniality, but only eight years later, becomes a "gentleman' candidate" with high political ambitions his loudly proclaimed American citizenship became am embarrassment, and he hasty had a biographical paragraph inserted in the Adelaide Advertiser: "Mr. King O'Malley is a native of Canada and was born on July 2, 1858. He was educated in the United States…."

For ever more and almost to the day fo his death, there were challenges and enquires as to where he was born. The "King" found it necessary to devise a standard statement giving his place of birth as Stanford Farm, Canada, and that his parents were British subjects born in the United Kingdom and offered an affidavit to that effect whenever he he found it necessary prove his right to be a member of The Australian parliament. Of course, neither his statements nor the affidavit rang true to enemies or his friends, and both had a well grounded belief that O' Malley was probably an American citizen by birth. Although he was finally brought to admit, long after he retired , that his actual place of birth and circumstance of his birth continued to be shrouded in uncertainly, it was more like that in truth he himself was unsure.

A period of twenty nine years passed by between the time O' Malley left the United States for Australia and when he made his only return visit in 1917. In the question of his birthplace it had become so important that he told friends that he had made an effort to obtain a birth certificate in his travels. When he returned to Australian without one he explained that the lack of a registration of his birth was not unusual as the frontier regions of the United States and Canada in the regions early history. So the absence of birth certificates were not uncommon at the time.

It seem more like that O' Malley was a native of Kansas and tells more of the origin of his raconteur stories of the wild west, his flamboyant dress style, and "ten gallon" that became his trademark as a cowboy. It is true that throughout his lifetime he maintained friendships with peoples of the Lawrence and Pawnee county for many years in his adult life. He had admitted late in life that he knew little of the history of his family: "…I know little of the history of the O' Malley family because we never bothered, good, bad or indifferent…" He seems to have barely know his father and according to his own account, the father was killed in Civil War, and as a young man saw little of his mother, let alone his brother and sister he is reputed to have had. When his father died, according to O' Malley he was seven at the time. The family then broke up and he was sent to live with his uncle and aunt in New York, and seems never to have seen his mother or siblings thereafter.

It is difficult to tell how much such a separation effected him but is probably a contributing factor to his characteristics in his adult life. So it was not until he became a prominent political figure in his adopted country that he was conscious of the need for family connections and thus he began to invent relationships with prominent people in the United States. In 1910, after twenty two years in Australia he suddenly embarked on a passion for correspondence with a prominent O' Malley legal family in Buffalo, New York and continued the practice of writing to them for the next thirty years. Over the years he also wrote various introductory letters under his offical   government letterhead to introduce friends and acquaintances who were visiting America, to Justice

James and Edward O' Malley and to their sister Mary, the Clinical Director of St. Elizabeth Hospital in Washington D.C. on the basis of being cousins. He also claimed to be related to the well known New York merchant, Edward Malley, and entertained his son-in-law, Lt.Malley-Keyes, during WW 1.

To a great degree his very feeling of inferiority was magnified by childish sensitivity and it is that stage of affairs which generated in him the insatiable abnormal craving for self approval and success in the eyes of the world. Still a child at heart, he cried for the moon, and the moon it seemed to him would not have him.

O' Malley spoke often of how his father was killed in the Civil War and his early years in New York living with uncle Edward and aunt Caroline, and how he learnt the skills of banking from his uncle who owned a small bank near Wall Street. He had been motivated by statement from his uncle that "money makes money" and at age fourteen joined the bank, being promoted to teller at sixteen and by age nineteen was allowed to make decisions on the granting of credit. But by the age of twenty two he had a fundamental disagreement with his Uncle on banking policy and left the bank for ever. But the idea of banking never left him and it served him well in his future occupations, and no doubt laid the seed for his later fight for the winning cause of a Commonwealth Bank of Australia which he contributed much in its foundation as a politician and long into his years of retirement.

His next move is proven as an Insurance salesman, for he gained notoriety far and wide in the frontier lands of the Americas as maker of fortunes for those who purchased policies from him. But to be sure the make believe career as a preacher is the one which was the myth he told most colourfully and the reason for his arrival down under. And he had no qualms in sprouting a quote or two about not only his favourite theme of the dangers of 'stagger juice ' but equally the inherent damage to health caused by smoking tobacco .

I am thoroughly satisfied that smoking
is detrimental to the intelligence of Australians
who I notice now are beginning to look sickly pale
and intellectually destitute. "

- King O' Malley

CHAPTER 2.

THE KING OF MIRACLES

Michael Angel made his way up a steep slope of the Blue Mountains above the plains of the Cayuse Nation, now called Oregon. He was working under the instruction of one, King O' Malley, the claimed founder and self appointed Bishop of a revivalist church-Waterlily Rockbound Church-the Redskin Church of the Cayuse Nation. O'Malley had met Angel in a tent settlement of natives internees, in a sly grog shop and convinced the newly sobered alcoholic to join his cause in helping his flock to cease the evil drink, to turn their mind to God and give up their gold and silver donations to the pockets the grandiose preacher for their fee for services rendered on God's behalf.

It was O' Malley's statue like habit to stand tall on the back of his horse drawn carriage drawing the attention of an ever swelling crowd of native Indian and white folk to his church revival meeting and fine oratory on the evils of what he called' stagger juice.' A tall, tawny haired, good looking man with sparklingly blue eyes, he drew the crowds with his loud proclamation on the evils of alcohol , the importance of sobriety and living a godly life of sacrifice for ones fellow man. It was as much as a spectacle of entertainment as it was a self seeking means of lining the pocket of this temperance preacher.

King invariably performed a miracle or two, and Michael Angel was his side kick in that regard so to speak. It works fine for a few months as Angel remained sober and did his Saturday night duty to climb the mountain and set a stick of dynamite under a tree and at the appointed hour, as O'Malley pointed to the mountain for a sign from God, Angel would light the fuse of the dynamite and run like hell down the mountain slope as it exploded, much to the amazement of the Indians and the humour of many a white folk who weren't so gullible. O'Malley had to all intent and purposes proved then existence of God's powers of explosive miracles by the time the 'Angel of God' returned puffing at the feet of the great man with yet another miracle of his powers of persuasion.
King would then tell the story of Michael Angel, being influenced by the Arch-angel Michael himself, or some reference to Angel's miracle cure, recounting how he lived before giving up the drink, what miracle

happened that changed his life, and Angel would endorse how he now lived a clean and sober life.

Of course the pattern of the entertainment miracle changed somewhat as O' Malley sometimes climbed the mountain himself to light a burning bush which could be seen from below, and he would return like Moses with chiseled words on a stone table that only he seemed to have the power to interpret. At other times he enlisted the services of some trumpeting travelling musicians who would blast away with celestial sounds from the mountain as a once more given sign was waved by the hand of God's messenger. O' Malley had, according to his own retelling later, worked the tribes of the Cayuse Native American tribes in the area in belief of his own interpretation of the Biblical text, but more to the point he was preaching of the dangers of that 'stagger juice,' and its evil effect on the nature of man. To be fair he was quite right about the native tribes who were known to act crazy once under the influence.

Whilst O'Malley, throughout his life in Australia, always preached of the dangers to humanity of his so coined ' Stagger juice, he also maintained that he had always been a teetotaller. It cannot be denied, but how he got to know so much about the need for handing over to a power greater than self being God, and allowing that power to work miracles, is the stuff of the Steps of Alcholics Anonymous which was not founded until the late 1930s in the United States by alcholics Dr. Bob Smith and Bill Wilson. Although an abstinence pledge had been introduced by churches as early as 1800, the earliest temperance organisations seem to have been those founded at Saratoga, New York, and in Massachusetts in 1813. So it's quite plausible that O' Malley had attendant a church rally or two during his upbringing in New York or later on his many trails across America as an insurance salesman.

However when it came to producing miracles to the Cayuse natives to justify the belief in God and the abstinence from 'stagger juice' he had chosen the wrong tribe and location to make his story plausible. The Cayuse were known for their bravery and as horsemen. They bred their ponies for speed and endurance, developing what is now called the Cayuse horse. No longer restricted to what they could carry or what their dogs could pull, they moved into new areas, traveling as far east as the Great Plains and as far south as California, to hunt, trade, fight, and capture slaves. The Indian savage of the day were often at war, but

mainly as peace prevailed at the end of the Civil War and gold had pe-
tered out, more white settlers moved along the Oregon trail were for-
mally trading with natives for ponies they bred. It was known by the
time the wild preacher man arrived that they had settled in a Native reserve. It was late 1880s that O'Malley pulled in as the self proclaimed
man of God himself, and he earned a fair living from his oratory to
those now peace loving people. But he had to have moved on to make
a living and it seems that the location of the church he found by his own
admission was located below a mountain range in what would have
been around Kansas territory. It was not the wandering tribes of the
Cayuse that he would have preached to there.

If O' Malley's story has some plausibility, it is more than likely Pawnee
tribes of the Central Plains that historically lived in Nebraska and
northern Kansas but today are based in Oklahoma that he spoke of. The
Pawnees had kept a right to hunt buffalo on their vast, ancient range
between the Loupe, Platte and Republican rivers in Nebraska and south
into northern Kansas, now territory of the United States. They had suffered continual attacks by the Sioux that increased violently in the early
1840s. After encroachment by white settlers, the Pawnees ceded their
territory to the U.S. Government in the 1800s and were removed from
Nebraska to what is now Pawnee County in 1875. This would have
been the time and place that the so called creation of O' Malley's'
founding the revivalist church of "the Waterlily Rockbound Church- the
Redskin Church of the Cayuse Nation had transpired."

It seems the church was destined for great things and was welling in
popularity to the local tribes and white folk settlers who eked out a living from the land until misfortune struck in an unexpected way. It was
the night that Angel turned back to the drink and spoilt the whole 'kit
and caboodle' of O' Malley's temperance movement. Angel had forgot
to climb the mountain to set the dynamite and explode it on the given
signal from below the hill top by O' Malley in his proclamation of
God's miraculous workings. Instead Angel stumbled in to the Church
assembly and made his way to the the wagon where The King stood
preaching of the brotherhood of man. Angel still felt it his duty to tell
the O' Malley's message of his sobriety even though he was blind
drunk. O' Malley immediately sat him down and chastised him on his
fall from grace in the midst of the crowd. Always quick to cease the oc-

casion irrespective of circumstance, The King rained supreme and preached a litany of the dangers and evils of ' sagger juice,' using the now sleeping Angel as an example of such a fall. He summed it all up with then fact that God had not produced a miracle that evening because Angel had fallen from grace. The mishap would have past into the ether if it wasn't for the fact that Angel blotted his copy book and the O' Malley reputation once again.

King's prime purpose was to gain the local land without the need for paying for it by having the approval of the authorities for it to be proclaimed sacred ground. However, Mr. Angel after being sacked by O' Malley become drunk again in Denver ad revealed the whole story of the so called miracles to a newspaper reporter. There was no option but for O' Malley and his now band of 'religious friends' to leave as quickly as possible before the irate locals run them out of the territory. So they quickly packed their belongs and headed into the desert plains leaving nothing but dust and empty pockets of locals that were duped by the con man. Among his followers were a middle age women and beautiful young niece called, Rosy Wilmot who volunteered to play the harmonium at the meetings. So it came to pass that Rosy fell in love with 'The King' but didn't go with him when he was forced to high tail it out of the place. However Rosy had been with her mother and became terminally ill. So King returns to Rosy's house in Georgia and there they married. O' Malley, there is no doubt was one of most gifted raconteurs of his day and whilst this story has an air of plausibility and was believed by many of his acquaintans, those self same people disbelieved much else of what he said.

It is the irony of his life that this story is now remember when much of his solid achievements are now forgotten. The story, though fascinating, matching both the public image and not so scrupulous personality of O'Malley does not stand up to scrutiny and is most probably false. That so many of his friends believe the story is most likely due to the character of its narrator. The story was set in the panhandle country of Texas and the adjoining regions of New Mexico, Oklahoma and Kansas, but O' Malley on only one occasion became precise about it when he wrote to a friend, of many years towards the end of his life. In the letter to Leslie Jauncey, in 1945 he said: "I got a letter from Brother Dooling telling me that he flew to San Diego from Texas to Washington. If he had looked to his left he would have seen the peaks of the Coradilla Mountains where the Angel Mornea appeared and gave the crystals out of which we gathered the story for the Waterlily Bible. He passed our sacred ground, far more sacred than Jerusalem or Nazareth because the modern Waterlily scriptures came from there."

It seemed that in O'Malley's imagination at the time suffered some delusions of grandeur representing the magic vision of some majestic place and non existent scriptures. A close examination of maps of the area fails to show any trace of the Coradilla Mountains and the Panhandle itself is a particularly flat plateau scored by wide river beds. He had his mention in a part of his story that his disciples had taken hand written pamphlets from door to door is inherently unlikely. Even now the place is conspicuous for its lack of towns and villages and in the 1880s was largely dominated by unfenced cattle ranges. O' Malley's flair for dramatic language in naming the church, with the exception that he had hoped to attract local Indians as well as white settlers, was singularly ill chosen for it was obviously inappropriate for the Apaches of the Panhandle country and the Sioux Indians who lived there.

The whole story of the Waterlily Rockbound Church-the 'Redskin Church of the Cayuse Nation' is inherently improbable and the fact that it was believed by so many astute people is a tribute to the characters and personality of its author- so far removed from the common experience and scepticism of the many who were suspended in amazement in his presence whenever he told this mythical tale. For it is a fact that the Waterlily Rockbound Church name was changed in 1937 by O' Malley to the 'Temple in the Cayuse nation,' and in that it did hold some element of truth. For in the period between 1884 and 1888 O'Malley and some of his friends were engaged in preaching activities - in a cause which was always closer to his heart than any religious zeal. He had in 1884 became converted to the cause of the temperance movement- or rather probation and for the remaining sixty nine years of his life he was a strong opponent of what he coined as 'stagger juice.'

It is a strong possibility that his cause of temperance probably took place in Lawerence, Kansas when O'Malley was with shorthand writer and typist D.C. Kennedy who travelled with him in Lawrence Pawnee country and in Topeka as well as Seattle. O' Malley knew the countryside very well, perhaps from his childhood memories too, but it was more than from business acquaintance that Kennedy had written to O' Malley in Melbourne. For at the time of his traveling preaching about probation O' Malley had been involved with a Grace O' Donnell and the affair was still unresolved when he had hastily departed from America under a cloud of illegal activity. In 1888 Kennedy wrote to his friend: [My advise to you is to marry her if you can, and get yourself financially fixed. It is evident from what they tell me, that she has a liking for you, and you are following a foolish course to let that opportunity go by without an effort to profit by it. Two or three hundred thousand would reconcile you to a much less attractive person than she appears to be, but you are such queer devil, I don't know whether you will think seriously of this proposition or not.]

Kennedy's letter seemed to be accurate in his description of O' Malley as a 'queer devil,' For he had a remarkably ambivalent attitude to women., for he simultaneously idealised and dislike them, always fought hard for the betterment of their condition, but at the same time felt uncomfortable in their presence. It is a testament to the loving fortitude of his later wife Amy who was by his side throughout their long marriage to the end of his days. In any event it would have been quite out of character for O'Malley to have married Grace O' Donnell for her money. Never the less he had a strong sensual side to his nature which caused him endless trouble in later years, and this is evident from a final paragraph in Kennedys letter; for the shorthand typist seemed to sum him up more than anyone else. "Well I don't know what else to say to you…except to admonish you gains the temptations of the flesh. I do not expect you to lead a virtuous life; you couldn't do that you villain you; but keep yourself within reasonable bounds".

The various conflicting episodes of the period of O'Malley's life in the establishment of the Waterlily Church has been told in many forms but the most authentic was that of Dorothy Catts near the end of his life. He had told her that when travelling in the south west of the United States in the mid 1880s he learnt that religious bodies were eligible for substantial land grants in Texas to establish community settlements. He was not connected to any church but construed the idea of founding one so that he and his followers could acquire free land. So moving to PanHandle country in Texas he set about to establish a church. He quickly gathered a few disciples but found he needed something more if he was to succeed. Obviously the best way was to arrange some miracles to occur so that it would be apparent that the new church had the blessings of God, and meeting a man who surprising was named Angel, he arranged, with some suitable payment, to produce various miracles as circumstances demanded. A few of his trusted friend were taken into his confidence and so they worked to write pamphlets and had taken them from door to door to get people interested. The meetings then took place under cover of darkness, often in front of a mountain, and mounted on a wagon O' Malley preached the brotherhood of man. And as iI previously mentioned from time to time he would whip up the enthusiasm of his followers, miracles were arranged; on occasions with the sound of trumpets or an explosion on the mountain or a great fire would appear. All was going well until a drunk Angel having been paid off told the Denver newspaper reporter of the falsehood and trickery of O' Malley's church.

Well the rest dear reader, you may think you know, but for the fact that O' Malley had a caveat to his story. For one of the unsolved mysteries of O' Malley's life is how he arrived in Australia. For whilst he had possibly left America for Australian shores to escape the law, his story of the Church and his arrival down under differed a great degree to the reality. In Kings own words he told how his Rosy had contracted Tuberculosis and the bacteria attacked her lungs, kidney, spine, and brain and could have infected everybody who came in contact with her. When Rosy died he had left the church in the care of his disciples as he too had come down with the TB infection which effected his lungs. He was advised to head to London, and there he consulted a Harley Street specialist who could not help him so he returned to San Francisco where he was given six months to live. Sitting despondently on a park bench one day he met a sailor who told him to go to a place called Rockhampton in Australia where the climate would cure him.

On the advise of the sailor he found a ship heading for Queensland, and after much argument with the ships Captain he was at last granted permission to board ship with his coffin, to head to Port Alma, near Rockhampton. So late in the 1880s a desperately ill O' Malley at his last extreme breath arrived at the tiny Port Alma. Seeing his failing condition two fisherman took him up the coast a short distance and put him ashore on a deserted beach at Emu Park. too ill to care anymore about his survival, he found a cave and crawled into it to die. Hours later he awoke find a tall aboriginal looking down on him. Moved by pity,

Coowonga by name, cared for the sick man for two years in his own rough bark shelter and restored him to health with native herbs and bush tucker consisting mainly of Burdekin plums fresh fish and kangaroo meat. To pass the long days the sick man read his bible and small editions of the classics and learnt to speak Coowonga's language.

Finally cured but by no means fully recovered he regretfully left Coowonga and set out to walk to Melbourne some 1500 miles away to the South. After being delayed by his illness, he reached Sydney where he sold insurance to a number of the most prominent citizens of the day. Then with growing strength and renewed confidence he strode on to Melbourne and success.

This was the story often told by O'Malley with many embellishments in the telling of his early days and his arrival in Australia. Of course it is just a story and not an absolute statement of fact. It holds no more credence than the tale of the Waterlily Church, nor the fact of a non existent wife Rosy and how she died, for there are no records to prove nor disprove the stories, but it was all widely believed by the impressionable to whom O' Malley always believed to be larger than life. It is reasonably certain that O' Malley left the United States in perfect health in 1888 and his first recorded public appearance in Australia was at the Melbourne   Centennial Exhibition which opened on the 1st August 1888 and closed on 31st January 1889. While the exhibition was in progress he was a frequent visitor , and often made impromptu speeches to the press room being a picture of health and great vigour. There was only a maximum period of twelve months or less for O' Malley to travel to Queensland to be cured of tuberculosis and walk the fifteen hundred miles to Melbourne.

Instead of the harrowing and heartbreaking story he told, it is probable that, in good health but in trouble financially, he fled from the United states to Australia, landing possibly in Melbourne, then the main city of Australian colonies, towards the middle of 1888. As no extradition treaty existed between the Australian colonies and the United States, O' Malley was safe and able to go about the business he new best-selling insurance. Keeping in contact with Kennedy back in Seattle, he told him, of the progress of the Fire Dispatch Company which he had set up in Melbourne, apparently as an adjunct to his insurance business which he now conducted on behalf of Equitable Life Insurance. Significantly there was no indication that he sold insurance for his former employer, the Home Insurance Company of America.

By the end of 1888 he was already well established in the city which was to be his home for most of the sixty five years he spent in Australia and was to become a public figure. Long after his arrival in 1939, a former press man recalled the impression created by O' Malley in his frequent visits to the press room at the Centennial Exhibition:

"Amongst others who frequented the press room…were Phil May… and King O' Malley…We were frequently entertained by exhibitors and sometimes held socials on our own, at which King was usually called upon for a stump speech. He readily acquiesced in his well known wild and wooly style, usually turning pop up in a grey frock coat and tall grey hat. But on one occasion when he was celebrating the victory of a Republican candidate as President on the 1889 election he turned up in spotless lavender raiment, even to his gloves, and insisted in shouting the Press Room."

Business in Melbourne was not as lucrative as he had hoped, so he moved to Hobart Tasmania in 1889, where he quickly made friends at Cascade and soon become well known in the Debating Society. A year later in 1890 he was addressing a public meeting at New Norfolk on the subject of home rule for Ireland- a topic of continuing interest to him and on which he later corresponded with people in Ireland. In June of 1890 whilst living in Elizabeth Street he gave his occupation as 'expounder' and became a freemason where he later practised the craft in South Australia. Surprisingly though, there is no evidence that he ever sought to use the craft and make business of it in his ordinary day life.

O' Malley's real talents as Insurance salesman were nor wasted in Hobart, but to add to his status he adopted a brand this time, the style and title of 'Travelling Commissioner of the Equitable Life insurance Company of New York.' Tasmania in the early 1900s had a population of 170,000, and the amount of insurance in the city of Hobart was soon at saturation point. So possibly at the end of 1890 King headed for the wild west coast of the country on a small coaster cargo ship which plied regularly around the coastline. He landed in early summer at the primitive harbour of Trails Bay, then he walked the twelve miles in 'mud almost up to his neck' (King's words) to a newly bustling township of Zeehan.

The township of Zeehan was named after the Dutch explorer Abel Tasman's ship, the Zeehan. In 1882 silver-lead ore was discovered near Mount Zeehan, but the town's development was slow, transport problems hampering early mining activity. It was rough terrain in its primedays with steep mountain overpasses and coastal jungle like growth making it undergrowth almost impregnable. The countryside deterred all but the most adventurous prospectors. But in the last days of 1882 Frank Long pegged out the first claim on the Zeehan field after discovery a lead sulphur outcrop and in 1884 the first building, a paling hut was erected in what soon became a town of 10,000 people. When O'-Malley arrived six years later the rough track to anchorage at Trail Bay was still Zeehan's main outlet to the world. It was in this new world of wild adventurerous men, and equally wild women that King O' Malley thrived and obvious hoped he would do as well as he had selling insurance on the Pacific Coast of America.

When King O'Malley left his uncle's banking business in 1880, he launched himself on the world equipped with good looks, a persuasive silver tongue, boundless confidence and the the ability to make his own way in the world. It was to be some eight years later that a world wise man would step ashore in Australia in 1888 and in those years he honed the experience on which he drew from the rest of his life. It was that character of his full development of personality that both amused and infuriated Australians for his sixty years as businessman, politician and ultimately retiree.

It was by a chance encounter in the streets of New York that turned O'Malley from a banking career to insurance salesman. By his own account this was accidental: One day a middle age man attracted Kings attention. *"That man seemed to have reached a position of affluence and importance."* King had murmured to himself. King was sitting on a sidewalk seat contemplating his next career move when the man passed by. So he stood up and followed until the older man entered the doors of a fine new building, the head office of a well known insurance firm. King went inside and here he saw evidence of an efficient and successful business concern.

CHAPTER 3.

THE WHOLE WORLD FOR SALE

Although the insurance business was then a century old in the United Stated it still had twenty more years before it reached its first thousand million dollars worth of life insurance sales. It would be an industry that was racked with scandals in which policy holders lost large sums of money from carpetbagger like practices of salesman, erroneous business practice by the insurance companies and financial loss through investment decisions of which due diligence had not been completed prior to decision making. As luck would have it the young King O'Malley was the best the industry had recruited and both his banking experience and his quick skill at closing sales made him one of the best of what the industry had to offer.

The record of the company O' Malley represented was never stated by him publicly in Australia, but it appears he was first accepted and trained by the Home Insurance Company, for which he worked for many years. The records of his life insurance career in New York have seemingly disappeared, and that is probable because so many banks and insurance companies closed their doors or went into voluntary bankruptcy during the depression years of the 1930s.

It seems King did not stay long in New York and soon moved to Wichita, Kansas, the region of his imagination and formative years before the age of reason. He may have believed it would make his task easier in its pioneering days, but it must have been a hard place to sell insurance and it seems unlikely that he made much money. By his own account he tried to advertise himself and hired a sign writer. One morning in the streets of Wichita township a large calico sign appeared stretched across the street bearing the legend: "The Whole World For Sale By King O' Malley."much to the surprise of the passers bye.

O'Malley, in a short while had expanded his insurance practice to the sale of real estate to pioneers, farmers and towns folk. It appears that whilst he did not do so well in Kansas there were other compensations for such a gorgeous man whose quick wit and smooth tongue saw him on the road again. In reading the character of personalities of the west of those time, a percipient reporter wrote of King in 1910 about his former days in the USA, before his arrival in Australia and embarking on a political career he had embraced here.

There in the life insurance work O'Malley's imagination could be given full play. He became a canvasser and travelled all over America persuading people to insure their lives. He saw all phases of American life from the millionaire down to the tough and the hobo. He got to know them all and his observations then provided him with the wealth of material from which he weaves his reminiscences and experiences now. But he was a successful canvasser. His ultra-friendly manner, his volubility, his inability to know when he was beaten all stood in good stead and he became known from New York to San Francisco, from the cotton country of the east to the alkali deserts in the West, as the king of insurance men. Arizona, Texas, Nevada were all swarming with wild picturesque figures in those days. they all imprinted themselves on O'Malley's brain. He modelled himself on the cowboy of the western plains, and adopted the cowboy-pose and the cowboy manner as the disguise he carried with him through life.

Somewhere in his travels O'Malley found it lucrative to transfer his insurance agency from The Home Life Insurance Company to The Equitable Life Insurance Company of New York, and thereafter in the USA and in his life insurance career in Australia he remained one of their most successful insurance men. Although O'Malley's foundational career in his early years was in the sale of life insurance throughout the American States, he also had quite considerable success in the sale of real estate, and about 1884 became converted to the cause of temperance, or rather probation which lasted for the remaining sixty nine years of his life. Although he conducted most of his insurance and political business in hotels he always refused a drink, although this did not stop him 'shouting' the bar. It is quite probable that his cause for temperance took place in Kansas, possibly Lawerence, when O'Malley was with Kennedy. A born crusader, he was not content to just preach the cause but become involved in the politics of probation, first in Kansas, which ultimately became the first 'dry' state, and then in 1886 in the campaign to introduce probation to Oregon. During this time he took to being a journalist and produced a newspaper 'The Fighter', a probation newspaper. There is no evidence that it ever came of anything. The provincial newspapers of the time were vigorous in their editorial style and contempt of the laws of libel. Editorials in the Arizona Kicker provided O' Malley with a course in training of personal inventive rants. In March 1887 the newspaper published an editorial which, apart from its lack of humour, was a veritable model for some of the onslaught O' Malley was to make on his later political opponents in Australia.

All our readers will bear witness to the fact that we have exercised the greatest patience in being the slurs and taunts of our esteemed weekly contemporary. On three different occasions we have ben perfectly justified in killing him, but we restrained our hand because we know he owed two compositors money, which they would lose if he went underground... Our lo-eared, lop shouldered, knock-kneed, slob-sided, ramshackle, bald-headed, poverty striven, cross-eyed, web-footed, toothless old contemporary with an average circulation of 217 copies weekly is no match for our tens of thousands (see our sworn statement)....Thus we do confound, paralyse, upset, break in two, and knock out the human hyena wise spiteful soul would blacken our private character before this community and with the fair reputation of an angel in female clothes. Words fail to express our contempt for this human monster but no advances will be made in our advertising rates.

It was apparent that O'Malley's unsuccessful journalistic efforts were concerned with furthering the cause of probation, which ultimately was introduced in Kansas in 1881 and justified his cause. The fact that he was not a successful editor or journalist was not surprising as his literary skills were poor even in entering into the low level of journalism in the American West of his time. The Kings real skill lay in his ability of speech. Recognising this fact, he concentrated his crusading efforts on preaching the cause of temperance to the accompaniment of Moody and Sankey hymns in small towns of the midwest and pacific states. In the middle 1880s probation was the issue of the day in Oregon and Washington State, and at every opportunity O' Malley spoke to 'brothers and sisters' of the cause in Seattle, Salem, Portland and small towns. Finally the issue was put to vote and the the result was a defeat for the advocate of probation. Despite this best efforts O'Malley's mood was upbeat and gracious in defeat, and according to a reporter at Wallula Junction in Washington State … he was like the grid-iron player Mark Tapley, gracious in defeat.

However important the temperance movement was to him he had to make a living. So he combined selling insurance and land, especially on the West Coast, and preach temperance whenever the opportunity offered itself. He was in his late twenties at the time, tall, handsome, possessing fluent, but easy manner and already known widely across the Americas as a raconteur. A reporter who met him on the West Coast about 1887 described him as: *King O' Malley of San Fransisco than whom there is not a more glib, single-handed talker on the coast...of course he is an insurance agent but that does not detract from his reputation as one of the brightest wits and most agreeable gentleman on the road.*

It seems at the time that O' Malley used San Francisco as his home base but it would appear that he roamed from San Diego in the south to the Canadian border. Despite his abilities he had many ups and downs financially in both insurance and real estate on the West Coast, but it was to lay the seed for his undeniable foundations for the considerable estate he acquired in Australia. He recognised his ability as showman and always keeping his name before the public, using in Seattle-the same calico banner stretched across the street offering the earth for sale, and inserting bizarre advertisements in local newspapers like: *The Equitable Life is the noblest and greatest Financial Temple of Equation ever erected by the genius of mortal man. King O' Malley.*

An intriguing question concerning O'Malley's activities at the time was whether or not he was married when moving up and down the Pacific Coast, perhaps with his wife in San Francisco. His story of the Waterlily Church and his marriage to Rose Wilmot who seemingly acquired tuberculosis and died was to all intentional purposes a myth of O' Malley's making. So to his becoming infected and seeking a Harley Street Specialist in London's advise for a cure. He always appeared to be the picture of health in his travels in the Americans and on his arrival in Australia which although the immigration records are obscure, he was reported to have been seen at Fremantle docks on arrival in early 1888 in the picture of health. So before we put to rest his stint telling of the Waterlily Church, the non existent wife Rosy, and his being cured by an Aboriginal of TB whilst living in cave near the beach near Rockhampton in sunny Queensland, a little more needs to be aired.

When he married in 1910 be described himself as a widower, and over the next forty three years of his married life referred from time to time to Rosy, saying, when his wife Amy refused to do something 'Rosy would have done that.' Despite the harrowing story of Rosy's death as an expectant mother in pain and sorrow, it is doubtful Rosy ever existed outside of O' Malley's imagination. Quite possibly he built the story from the many female acquaintance he come in contact with on his many travels selling insurance and real estate. At the time of his so called establishment of The Waterlily Church and his reported marriage to Rosy, he could not have been in two places at once. At that time (1883-4) he was living in Kansas and up to 1887 was banking money and presumably living in Corvallis, Oregon- and he said he established himself in banking in Georgia, worked in real estate in Virginia, worked for the election of James Blaine as President, and went to England, Ireland, Scotland, Wales, France, and Germany. In his last statement in that that regard he said he studied banking in Berlin. This was the same period he was establishing himself as an insurance and real estate man on the Pacific Coast, so the improbability of his story becomes apparent.

As a travelling insurance agent O' Malley had little of the status he always craved , and he had not been successful as a journalist or advocate of probation. But towards the end of the decade his financial position had improved so that by March 1887 his bank passbook showed a balance of $1891.19 and he had acquired property in Seattle which was rapidly increasing in value. This he retains for many years. But his hasty departure from USA to Australia when he seemingly was financially sound has always been under a cloud. Selling insurance undoubtedly brought in a steady income but it seems he made more money in real estate. So his sudden deposit of $1891.19 in his Corvallis account lends itself to speculation and perhaps was the catalyst to his hasty retreat to Australia.

O' Malley, after his final defeat at the elections of 1917 headed off to America after being absent from there since 1888 when he came to Australia. There had always been much speculation as to what deed he had been involved in to cause him to turn his back on the world he once knew. He was apparent in a state of flux as to his future in Australia, but he must have felt it was safe for him to go back to America in 1917.

On board ship returning there he wrote to Amy, his wife: I am real glad that I got defeated in the election, otherwise we would have lost the American estate that is worth so much. I shall reorganise the whole thing and then we may sell out in Australia if the climate is not too bad.

It was apparent that he was home sick for all things American at the time, but he still professes that he was a Canadian citizen without any proof of being so. It was only late in life that he acknowledged he was born of American parentage. Whether or not his newly acquired affluence was gained honestly is another matter and is connected with his attitude to conventional morality. His method of gaining sales was always of showmanship and quick wit, and the promise of the stability of his "Temple of financial glory. The Equitable Life Insurance Company of New York" As it turns out, and has always proven to be so; despite the trickery that abounds with mankind in the handling of money it has always been said that money is the root of all evil.

In the early months of 1892 O'Malley continued to sell insurance in the north of Tasmania, travelling through the small towns and villages blowing his veritable trumpet about himself and Equitable Life. He was found to be so successful that if another salesmen found he had been in town he would move on knowing there was no business worth the writing after'The King' had been there.

Towards the end of 1892 the attractions of Tasmania weakened as the potential market for insurance had been exhausted and King O'Malley once more looked to the mainland. He left Launceston in October and it waa apparent that he left with such short notice that it was rumoured he had fled to escape debtors. This is most unlikely as he shortly afterwards was able to invest in property in Melbourne, but he felt strongly enough to dispel the rumours by having denial inserted in the Launceston Examiner. It not only seemed like that a good insurance agent in a large society gave his reason that he was on his way to visit the World Exhibition in Chicago, but is was more the likely that he already had his eye on entering Tasmanian politics at some date in a future election.

It was a policy of the insurance company of O' Malley's time to help with the expenditure of their travelling salesmen with reimbursing various costs in their efforts to secure business. In O' Malley's early travels in Australia's wilderness, he submitted his reimbursement of expenses sheet to Head Office and included the cost of a 'ten gallon hat' as necessary expenditure. The company knocked this back as being a matter of dress and therefore not claimable. Put out by this O' Malley resubmitted the claim with a note that it protects him from the hot Australian sun whilst in the course of his duty. The approving officer sent him a reply to the effect that it still was not claimable. On the following months claim O'Malley's claim for expenses was approved in full. On King's next appearance in Head Office the approval officer approached him and stated; "I see your claim for the cowboy hat was not there in your last claim.? O' Malley replied: "Oh! it's there all right, you just can't see it."

On another occasions in his mainland selling days O' Malley, whilst riding along mid western trail, come across a cattle drive. The head drover was resting under a tree for a break from the midday sun, whilst his Aboriginal stockman kept the herd of cattle quietly grazing nearby. O' Malley attempted to sell the stockman a life insurance policy, but was quickly stopped in his tracks: " I don't believe in life insurance mate." he replied. " I don't need it as I am not afraid of anything, least of all death." O' Malley with a curious look on his face asked: "Surely there is something you are afraid of."

"Well yes," the drover said: "I am afraid of getting gored by one of those steers over there when they get their horns tangled, I have to go an untangled them." The King quickly extracted a proposal form from his pocket and replied; " We have just the police here, it's called a 'death by goring policy,' and should you die by such an event we will pay out the sum of 10,000 pounds to your next of kin. And for no extra cost we will throw in death by any other causes." The policy was duly written with a notation of death by goring and any other cause and was accepted by the life insurance company. The story appeared in the next months copy of the Insurance News bulletin as an example of another of O' Malley's persuasive selling ability.

Another story transpired about the time of O' Malley on a political mission in Tasmanian. An article in the Hobart ewspaper the Tasmanian mail wrote of a certain lady Mrs. Delaney, a middle-aged lady of Irish origin, who had never lost her accent. She was renowned for her lightning-fast wit, and razor sharp tongue. Each day, she left her small shop in the small hamlet of Rhyndaston in the care of a young boy, boarded the north-bound express train, and travelled to the next station at Parattah. Her journeys were always free of any charge, as it was commonly believed that, many years ago, she had noticed a wash-away on the railway one stormy day. Hearing a train approaching, she took off her red flannel petticoat, and ran towards the train, waving it madly to warn the engine crew of the danger. For saving the train and many lives, she was given the privilege of free rail travel for life. Mrs Delaney would set up a stall and sell to the train passengers, who were getting rather peckish by then, produce such as apples, sometimes of questionable quality. O' Malley's northbound express train train from Rhynanston to its arrival at Parattah had stopped there and passengers would get a chance to stretch their legs whilst the trains engine crew took on water for the steam locomotives and cleaned its fire. All who knew O'Malleys wealth of repartee had not yet encountered the likes of Mrs Delaney's good nature and quick wit. She was always fresh and cheery, and is as much an institution at Parattah station as the refreshment room. She hated anything like snobbery, and was never slow to check. According to the press article of the day she gave two examples of that last week, when she was approaching a carriage occupied by a lady and gentleman looking as if they were on their honeymoon. *"You can't go in there"*, said the young man standing on the footboard.*"Oi can't, can't oi; an' how's that?"* "Because it's engaged", he replied.*"Engaged it is, is it? By the looks o' you, you ought to have engaged a cattle truck!"*Of course, all bystanders laughed with the utter confusion of the victim.

In another report, she entered a carriage compartment, in which a well dressed fellow was seated. At her approach, he drew up in the corner. Not being even slightly nonplussed, she flopped down, and placed her fruit basket and umbrella on the seat. Noticing he was annoyed, with her ready wit she said, *"Perhaps you would like it better if I were a gentleman?"* *"Yes, I would"* he replied. *"Be jabbers, now, that's strange. I was just thinking the same about you. There, now, me foine fellow."* Not even politicians were immune to her wit, in particular, one Federal member, by the name of "King" O'Malley.

One day, Mrs. Delaney became aware that someone of importance was aboard the express. She pleaded with a local resident to tell her who the guest of honour was, and was told not to embarrass the town with any of her sharp remarks. *"Oh, no, dearie, if you'll tell me who's on the train, I promise I'll be very well behaved, and I won't say a word"* So, she was told the V.I.P. was none other than "King" O'Malley, to which she expressed great excitement. Mrs Delaney was not one to stand quietly and discretely in the background. She turned many a head as she pranced from one end of the platform to the other, swinging her hips, swishing her long skirt, and calling out loudly. *"What do I care for 'King' O'Malley? What do I care for 'King' O'Malley? What do I care for 'King' O'Malley?"*

A commercial traveller braved the pouring rain at Parattah one day and dashed across the station platform to buy some of Mrs. Delaney's apples. These she put in a paper bag, which the traveller thrust into his coat pocket. He soon realised the lining was torn, as the apples landed on the platform. Hastily scooping them up, he rammed them into the pocket on the opposite side, but that one was no better, and the apples poured back onto the ground again. Red-faced with embarrassment, he was again retrieving the fruit, when the entire world learned of his misfortune. This was when a well known voice yelled, *"If you're as hole-y as all that, you art to be a praist!"*

On another occasion, "King" O'Malley again came off second-best, when he happened to be travelling in the same compartment with Mrs. Delaney. Giving Mrs. Delaney a prod in the abdomen, he said, *"And what are you going to call it?"* Not the least concerned, her immediate reply was, *"Well, if it's a boy I'll call it Patrick after the saint, and if it's a girl I'll call it Brigid after me mother, but if it's what I think it is, all piss and wind, I'll call it 'King' O'Malley!"* For once King O'Malley was lost for words.

The trail of then Travelling Commissioner of the Equitable life now disappears for a period of seven months until he turns up in Adelaide in May 1893. There is no indication of his actual whereabouts during that period but it is probably factual that he initially went from Tasmania to Western Australia. King O'Malley became quite wealthy through his insurance business and by investing in real estate in Melbourne. One could speculate that his real wealth to afford so many properties quite possibly came about by his seven months absence from the insurance world were it is assumed he hit the pay load by speculating in gold in and around Kalgoorlie during the Western Australia gold rush days. The pastoral life of this remote colony had been shattered in 1892 by the gold discovery of Boulder and the gold rush from eastern stated began in earnest. Miners of all ages and conditions poured through the port of Esperance heading for the booming goldfields of Coolgardie-Boulder.

Some miners made fortunes but the real money was made by those who speculated or lived upon the miners. Late in 1892 O' Malley had made his first visit to Kalgoorlie and was a frequent visitor there between October 1892 and May 1893. Miners would have been a poor risk for insurance and if O' Malley was on the goldfields at this time it is more likely that he made his money by speculation. In June 1901, only eight years afterwards, Melbourne Punch giving a pen portrait of the apparent eccentric member from Tasmania as able to say: When times were bad in 1893-4 in the city of Melbourne, O' Malley brought his West Australian savings to this new home base and brought up seven or eight decent little cottages, had them put in good order and has now a clear income of 200 pounds from them. His eccentricities are merely part of his capital.

However, his future was endangered in 1896 when his acquaintance from the United States, William Moorhead had tried to blackmail him by threatening to reveal the details of his life in America. O' Malley won a defamation case, but his past continued to remain a subject of speculation for the rest of his life.

O' Malley was not the one to stay in a mining town to long. From past life experience he knew all about the booms and bust of goldfields, having lived in America during the Californian Gold Rush and seen its decline a few year before hand. For whatever the attraction Kalgoorlie might be for making capital gains, it had little attraction for a prince among insurance salesman and for no obvious reasons he decided to settle in Adelaide for a time.

He was an alleged widower, perhaps disappointed for a second time in entering federal politics via a Tasmanian seat, he thrust himself upon the citizens of the sedate Adelaide. The phenomenon of an O' Malley of King's calibre the locals were totally unaccustomed. in the mind of the not so discerning locals here was a person they saw as an expert insurance salesman who waa also a fanatical supporter of temperance, a man of great ideas who lived a humble life in coffee palaces, great advocator of women's rights and their foremost supporter who yet remained a widower, a vociferous advocate of all things American who yet declared he was a loyal Canadian and strong supporter of labor ideals who would join the labor party and an man who hated the wealthy but himself was well off. An obvious Yankee of assertive manner, unknown to anyone in the city in mid 1893, an enigmatic personality but who bred distrust in Adelaide's elite circles, O' Malley was in three short years to become one of the city's best known characters and against all odds got himself elected to parliament.

When O' Malley arrived in South Australia it had just gone through a particularly unstable period and Downer had just emerged as Premier to see the colony to the next election. The fear that Victoria was trying to annex the Serviceton railway station on the border between the two colonies paled into the background as banks were collapsing, and large numbers of unemployed thronged through the streets of Adelaide. Politics then was more played on personalities than strict party guidelines. It was a perfect time for O' Malley to make his presence known for his future entry into a political career.

O'Malley, even in his illustrious career as an insurance salesman, reputedly gave his date of birth at various times as July 2,3 or 4 in the year of Our Lord 1854 or 1858 as the case may be. He ultimately settled in his own words as being born on July 4th, American Independence Day, and publicly gave his birthplace as Stanford farm in the Eastern township of Quebec, Canada, he was more than likely born at his parents farm at Valley falls, Kansas, or near Wichita. The Canadian birthplace suited his ambitions to become a Federal political as it justified his application as having a British colony and unwritten proof to enter the political arena in Australia. O' Malley had attempted and failed numerous times to win a seat or to find a party vacancy to gain entry to unleash his ambitions on the Australian people. So whilst still selling insurance in Adelaide, with no more than vacant thoughts of any other career, the desire to chance his soul purpose came as a result of the Hon. T Playford's, treasurer in the Kingston Government He had previously served two terms as Premier of South Australia (1887–1889; 1890–1892), and-departed the colony in April 1894 to become Agent- General in London.

O' Malley saw his opportunity to use the by-election as the initial catalyst to his publicity campaign with his eyes then firmly fixed on a career in politics. He had for a long time on his rounds in the street of Adelaide told the story of how he arrived in Australia, but the story varied to a great degree from the one he had told in Melbourne and in Tasmania when he resided there.

The king's story of the Waterlily Rockbound Church-the Redskin Church of the Cayuse Nations first bishop did not vary much , nor his story of his travels across the US selling insurance and real estate, but his landing in Australia, and his arrival in South Australia had a different twist when told in Adelaid. He claimed he had left after his wife died of TB in 1886, shortly after the birth of their first child and he said he had contracted the disease and in 1888 was given six months to live. He did not want to give the disease to his child, and on good advice to improve his chances of survival he set sail to Port Alma near Rockhampton, wandered the seashore and fell asleep on the beach. [And this is were his story varied to suit the Adelaide audience.] An Aborigine, Coowonga, carried him to a cave at Emu Park, saving him from drowning from the encroaching tide. So with his consumption arrested by open air camp life with the Aborigines, O' Malley said he then walked 1305 miles (2100km) to Adelaide, 'meeting notabilities en route in Brisbane, Melbourne and Sydney.' Time has proven with much research of social historian's that O' Malley, disgraced in Oregon over fraudulent insurance sales, arrived in Sydney abroad the SS Mariposa in July 1888, and in September travelled to Melbourne arriving dress flamboyantly in the picture of health.

O' Malley's insurance practices in Australia and in particularly in Adelaide were of the most honest kind. Although he was prone to overstate the virtues of his beloved Equitable Life Insurance company, the financial values and interest returns on the policies he wrote proved always to be true. He had acquired great wealth from his gold speculation in Western Australia and perhaps had a long term goal to settle in Melbourne long before he actually did.This is evident by his continual purchase of slum like dwellings in Melbourne. But ultimately renovated and repaired,he rented them all out at a fair cost to his tenants.

CHAPTER 4.

THE PREDACIOUS ROAD OF THE KING

The campaigning for the by-election of the right Hon. T. Playford's' seat he vacated due to his new London post drew four candidates Messrs Rees, Prod, White and Packman, to a noisy and riotous meeting at Norwood Town Hall in Adelaide on 2nd May. after each speaker had his speech punctuated by cheers, groans, and interjections, the chairman invited questions and several were accepted. However, the Chairman could not be heard above the din of the crowd. A drunken man made a disturbance, but with less stirring anger the candidates behaved disgracefully which made them unworthy of high office of which they craved. It was not just the reporter of the Register who was disgusted by their performance The paper of 5th May contained in its Electoral notices a seven inch advertisement addressed 'To The Sovereign Electors of East Torrens' and signed by King O' Malley. The Editor of the Register found the advertisement 'decidedly original' which was looked upon by the populous as decidedly understated. The notice read:

"After the Pandemonium Political Pow Wow' of the 2nd instant at Norwood I think that the infusion of more American blood into the Parliament of this commonwealth is essential to its existence and therefore I would regard with favour a proposal to stand as a compromise candidate on the Conditional retirement of all the other brethren.] If this raised a few eyebrows of the Registry readers they had a greater shock coming; for O'Malley preceded with his policy:

[While their policy is impregnated with Utopian dreams of mental visions, mine is founded upon the rock of endless duration; it is incontestable, non-forfeitable and indestructible. I am for the total annihilation of rowdy, hoodlum mules. Theatres and public halls where citizens gather to discuss political and other moral subjects should contain iron cages for the incarceration of the arrogant, ringtail, brainless mules who affect and shock the audience by their senseless vulgar braying at the speakers.These lineal descendants of salaam's ass, devoid of all psychological attainments of their illustrious progenitor, must be either reformed or muzzled... The mules who infest meetings with idiotic braying, driving good men out of political life, is an excrescence on the tree of liberty and a living menace to free institutions...All those who favour my candidature shall be entitled to front seat at my funeral.]

Whilst O' Malley drew the maximum amount of attention to his cause it did not encourage voters to change their desired course, and on 17 May Packman was duly elected without having to face an encounter with the rebound-able agent for Equitable life. Ever present advertising his ideas in the press, O' Malley finished the year with a final comment in the Register on Adelaide's Bishop Kennion's resignation to become the Bishop of Bath and Wells in the UK. [Apostolic Succession- In order to prevent any further spiritual friction in the church of England I am prepared to accept the position of Bishop, and insure all the brethren.- King O'Malley.]

No notice was taken of his generous offer and O' Malley had to resign himself to continuing to be the first Bishop of the Waterlily Rockbound Church. Apart from his regular articles in the press on the bank failures in the colonies in 1883, and his suggestions to both Governments and the public on the American system of banking and insurance, and the best practice and laws in that regard, none of his suggestions were accepted at the time.

It would be his most pet subject throughout his political life and his retirement years, but between 1884 and 1885 his interest spread on a number of different front. Female suffrage was always of interest to him, for he believed that one day it would be of benefit in his gaining female votes to his election objectives. Of course in 1885 the fact that the Queen assented to the Bill which had been passed, despite opposition by conservative members who failed to realise that women were likely to vote conservative. O'Malley had written many an article for this cause in the press, and was delighted when the female vote was enshrined into law. Months of debating time in parliament to bring the State Savings Bank under government control was fervently debated with legislation in train to prevent monopoly control of public housing. Each of these issues was well calculated to make O' Malley speak out but the letter and advertisement columns of the Adelaide newspapers were without contribution my him.

When the Hon.G.C. Hawker, a long standing sitting member for Adelaide died in May 1885 after a short illness, there was an immediate scramble for his seat. At the time O' Malley was absent from Adelaide, perhaps in Melbourne to check on the rental and renovation of property or back in Kalgoorlie on another speculation deal, so he seemed to show no interest in the election. A very Catholic Patrick McMahon

Glynn, who later became a great friend of O' Malley, in parliament and privately, won the seat .

It was obvious O'Malley was absent from South Australia at the time as no press coverage or advertising on female suffrage, liquor control nor the benefits of personal insurance appeared. It seemed at the time that whilst the Adelaide community was stabilising the prospects for insurance sales was not good, and King was mainly occupied in the buying and selling of mining leases.

As the life of Parliament neared its end in 1895, interest in parliamentary affairs wained for the time of endless debates, but then it began to revive. While Federation was on the back burner, it was never forgotten, and was accepted as inevitable. The issues of O' Malley's interest were aligned with the Labor party and its supporters even before he became a member. However he did not wish to be restricted by their rules and preferred to remain politically independent at that time. Whilst absent from South Australia for most of 1895 he was still domiciled there. So it was in January 1896 that he suddenly declared his intention of standing for Parliament. To do so he not only had to be a British citizen but to have resided in the colony and been on the electoral roll of some district within the colony for six months.

King O' Malley was known throughout Adelaide and its surrounds as a genial and successful insurance agent, and a teller of tall stories waxing lyrically and loudly in his American Irish brogue. He was above all a man who believed in self promotion and announcing his intentions in the press, as well as in his canvassing of insurance. The public may well have been amused at his announcement to enter parliament, especially if they knew of his various earlier announcements in Tasmania and South Australia. The King was as always in earnest, and the only thing that mattered to him was which electorate to stand for. He was not concerned about how many people might vote for him, for he now felt he had a mission beyond the selling of bonds and policies of his beloved great financial temple, The Equitable Life… and believed he would win.

So it was that 'the Register ' issue of 18th January reported King O' Malley was a candidate in the next election for the district of Encounter Bay, a sea side township about 80 kilometres (51 miles) from the centre of Adelaide. The boundaries of the electorate in selected centred housed the small towns of Goolwa, Port Elliott and Victor Harbour. It was not such an obvious choice for much of it was occupied by small farmers who were very conservative in outlook and apparently quite content with their two local member, John Kelly, a farmer from Bald Hills and Henry Downer, a solicitor of Adelaide. However,O' Malley was a frequent visitor to the area, and was quite popular with the locals in Goolwa and Victor Harbour. The landed gentry of the Strathalbyn area were not so kind. It was not until 27th February that the *Southern Argus* carried the first genuine advertisement from O' Malley.

[To the electorate of Encounter Bay
Ladies and gentleman- At the next general election I shall be a candidate for your suffrages, and during the campaign will gladly meet all worthy opponents in the arena of debate on the issues for your final judgement. King O'Malley]

Despite O'Malley not being able to prove his birth right to be a candidate for the election, and the fact that he had been on the electoral role for six months, even though he had not stayed that long in South Australia when moved to Western Australia to speculate on gold futures, he was duly accepted. He stood as an independent , surprising observers by topping the poll ahead of Willian Carpenter of the United Labor Party and sitting MP Henry Downer of the Australasian National league, and former MP Charles Hussey. The tall good looking flamboyant well dressed young man enjoyed strong support among the newly enfranchised female voters, who were sympathetic to his pro-temperance views.

At the opening of parliament in June 1896, O'Malley and seven others refused to take an oath of office and were refused their seats. They were eventually allowed to make affirmations and take their place. After his election O'Malley took up residence in a coffee palace on Hindley Street Adelaide, although he made frequent visits to his electorate. In Parliament, he concentrated on social matters, starting with a proposal to regulate barmaids, the use of which he regarded as a social evil. His attempt to amend a government liquor licensing bill to that end was unsuccessful. O'Malley next introduced a bill requiring seats to be provided for shop assistants, which also failed, followed by a successful motion calling for train carriages to be provided with lavatories and better lighting. A private members bill he introduced in 1897 eventually passed as the *Legitimation Act*

1898, allowing for the legitimisation of children born out of wedlock whose parents subsequently married. By this time, O'Malley had aligned himself with the government of Charles Kingston, declaring himself "on the side of the ministry" and calling Kingston "the greatest democratic leader this country had ever known". He strongly supported federation and in a series of parliamentary speeches championed the U.S. constitution as a model for Australia. However, little notice was taken of his views.

O'Malley was defeated for re-election in Encounter Bay at the April 1899 general election, with William Carpenter outpolling him by 14 votes and Charles Tucker outpolling both. The election was fought largely on the temperance issue, with Tucker enjoying the support of the Licensed Victorian' Association. Their supporters clashed on a number of occasions, culminating in a "near riot" at Goolwa the day after the election. A petition was subsequently lodged against Tucker's return, on the grounds that he had attempted to bribe electors. The result was declared void in July 1899 and another election ordered, which was equally acrimonious but resulted in a clear victory for Tucker against O'Malley.

The ever positive O' Malley was not aware at the time that his political career in state politics had been extinguished. He had in his time in the house, against all expectations excelled as a politician. Although not fully committed to labor principles he had continued to cherish his independent stance but his ideas were generally supported by labor movements. O' Malley's exaggerated similes and fervent adulation of all things American had many of his fellow members back his fervent demands for social reform and justice for the small man, and his support of women's rights, allowed him to build a partisan group of supporters who could see no flaws in him. The O' Malley that went down to Encounter Bay in March 1899 to campaign for another term in the house of State Parliament was by outward appearance the same tawny headed firebrand, but he was somehow more chastened, more cynical and had acquired the discipline to allow him to be one of the key figures in federal politics in the next two decades.

The loss of his seat in Encounter Bay to Tucker in the 1899 election meant for O'Malleys time for a South Australian seat in parliament was over. The Victorian election was not due until the end of 1900, so in the beginning of February 1900 O' Malley returned to his old haunts of Zeehan, as elections where about take place there and he new by past experience there that it was the obvious place to try again.

The *Zeehan and Dundas Herald* reported him as taking up residence in the new and impressive Grand Hotel and he expressed his surprise at the progress that had ben made in his absence. *The Mount Lyell Standard* of 1st February had reported that O' Malley was going to address the electors of Lyell constituency and the following day an anonymous correspondent wrote to the *Zeehan* and the *Dundas Herald* to ask if O' Malley was eligible to contest the election as he had only recently arrived in Tasmania a few weeks ago. This brought a reply the very next day that he could stand for selection, as the only qualification was the candidate be 21 years of age and a British subject, but he could not vote himself. Tasmania then was one of the most conservative colonies with limited social legislation, and it was typically a rural dwelling place engaged in agriculture. Already there was a population of over 20000 in the mining districts of the West Coast from Strahan to Waratah, many of whom had migrated from Victoria with radical ideas.

O' Malley knew from his South Australian campaigning experience that radical social reform frightened and alienated conservative farmers, so to seek votes he focused on the miners and labourers of the Mount Lyell area. A month before the election on 8th February, he opened his campaign with a long speech on aspects of social justice and economic reform to a very large crowd at the Queenstown Academy of Music. The crowd were drawn to this wild and woolly orator and even more so to his skill in self promotion. He stood tall, wearing a golden beard and moustache, an Abraham Lincoln like frock fiat, three decker tie with pin, very bad shirt style but well cut trousers, spotless tan boots and above all a very broad brimmed and tall hat, in a ten gallon caboose style- he was a picture of satirical elegance.

The King allowed his opposition candidates the opportunity to speak first and then he launched into his usual mixture of racy anecdotes and advanced ideas. He told the audience of his past history in politics and went with a detailed list of reform ideas he would fight to introduce if elected. From old age pensions for miners, to workers compensation for men disabled in the field and the placing of cushions on seats of second class carriages on the Zeehan rail trains, to free hospital, free education from primary school to university so that the right man might gain the right place in the country.

If he was elected he hoped to please the electors that he would ultimately gain the West Coast to support him for federal Senate seat. From there he would carry through old age pension reform and university tariff which would protect the workers of Australia against Europe influences. He had stated that: *He hoped to do more, to change the workers for being bonded slaves of monopolising greed to the partner in institutions they had made by their perspiration and labor.*

The Boar War in South Africa was the main item of public interest on the West Coast, as it was across Australia, but O' Malley choose to ignore it, possibly because he was pro-Boer, or it may have been because of his anti-military views, or perhaps because he thought it was irreverent to the issue of his election campaign. But his omission was certainly noted by his competitors and was the main contributing factor to his unseating an obviously patriotic Gaffney. Moving from settlement to settlement, from camp to camp in the final weeks of his campaigning, O'Malley worked hard to defeat his main rival but Gaffney in the end won by a surprising 318 vote difference.

It was O' Malley's third defeat in Tasmania. So he returned to Melbourne, but he was soon back in Tasmania. For the Commonwealth Bill for a Federal Parliament in Australia was about to pass the House in London. And on 1st May the following notice appeared in the *Mount Lyell Standard.*

[TO THE SUPREME ELECTORS

Gentleman- I have returned, notwithstanding the assurance of the wise know-alls to the contrary, and shall be a CANDIDATE for the FEDERAL HOUSE OF REPRESENTATIVES at the forthcoming Election, next September. I therefore trust no elector will promise his vote to any candidate until the candidate has proven the possession of the political knowledge essential for so important a position. I will be at Hynes' Store every evening for two weeks to put democracy on the roll. KING O' MALLEY

It seems O'Malley's activities between 1884 and 1887 were centred on speculative activities. It remains a mystery as to his sudden decision in 1888 to board a boat bound for Australia. If his story of the Church be founded and the TB he contracted has any element of truth unlikely, but to be sure, when he arrived here he was already a world wise thirty one year old who had seen many ups and downs in his life. He had the basic rudiments of banking and insurance which was to make him an expert in the councils of Australian labour, and a memorable man of outlandish words and phrases, and he soon became known for his widely publicised hatred of ' stagger juice' and promoting the dangers of tobacco smoking. He would soon enough walk the halls of parliament with hundreds of stories that he would tell over the next sixty five years of his life here, and he would gain financial prominence as a real estate investor too.

In 1895, two years after Paddy Hannan discovered gold at Boulder, the rail was laid from Perth to Kalgoorlie. As both the townships of Boulder and Kalgoorlie grew on the back of the gold rush, the rail link to Boulder was extended over the next 5 years. The late 1800s saw the Golden Mile Railway link become one of the busiest stretches of track in the southern hemisphere. During its peak in the gold rush, more than 100 steam trains moved through the stations of Kalgoorlie-Boulder each day, being equal to a train leaving the station every three minutes. It was the perfect atmosphere for a smooth talking loud mouthed story teller to rave on to mining prospectors at the ramshackle pubs that sprung up in those mining towns. And it is no doubt where King O' Malley gained his knowledge of prospective business opportunities and speculative gambles to be had on the young stock market based in Perth, and on the east coast in Sydney and Melbourne. For it was from those risk taking adventurers and not the actual mining of gold in which he gained the monies to build a portfolio of properties in Melbourne, and have enough left over to use to further his cause in advertising his talents to be the ultimate representative of the peoples of the mining areas of Tasmania's West Coast. Thus he launched his entry into campaigning for his seat as the Federal House of Representatives for the area in the pending Federal Parliament at its foundation.

By December 1900 other candidates were starting to make their preliminary speeches for a seat in the still unannounced date for the opening of Federal Parliament. O' Malley realised that his best bet was to focus most of his early activity on getting miners on the electoral roll for up to then not many had the right to vote. He made strenuous efforts even at considerable personal expense to achieve that aim. Over the next few months he moved from Strahan and Kelly Basin to as far as North West Coast going not only to the townships but to the camps and mines. As journalist B.C. Bursell reported at the time: [He would ride the small rail tracks to sawmills in all weather conditions, sometimes carrying a rope to secure himself on top of logs as there was no room in the engine room. The mines were miles away over mountains up to 3,000 ft (914.4 metres), there were no motor cars, cabs or horses and where he couldn't get on the rough bush trains he walked, still in his frock coat and 10 gallon hat. He was everywhere and wherever he was there was always fun… one of his jobs for a long time was to meet the men coming off shift at 7 am mostly in the rain saying: "Are you on the roll Brother, if not get on it, and you will want me because...etc etc]

The West Coast as pioneering societies were starved of entertainment and O' Malley with his wit and buffoonery always gave him a packed house. and intrigued his audience. On one occasion when questions by a member of the audience about his manner of unusual dress sense he responded with: 'If I had arrived here dress d in the ordinary way I'd never made myself known or had change, but by coming as I did every darn one of you knew me in a few days and liked me and now y success is certain.'

Often there were interjections at O'Malley's speech rallies but if he ever got really annoyed he would often reply to the interjectors in one of several different forms : ' If your brain were dynamite and exploded in the head of a Zeehan flea it would not even make it blink.' Then if this failed he would adopt a crude approach inviting the interjector to take a dose of epsom salts, go up a lane and get rid of his brains. However, these occasions were rare and normally the crowd was on his side and anxious to hear more of his ideas and his stories told in a way that they had never heard before.

The Commonwealth celebrations were held in Sydney at the beginning of January 1901 with enthusiasm that penetrated as far away as the west coast of Tasmania. However, less interest was shown in the forthcoming federal election and the candidates, who were coming forward in larger numbers, had to compete for the interest with local matters and the illness and death of Queen Victoria, as well as the dying embers of the Boar War in South Africa, and the news of the Boxer rebellion in China. So it was only on 29th March that the campaigning really got underway. So the candidates descended in force on the West Coast which contained 20 per cent of the votes, vital to a win for the chosen candidate. On the 6th March no fewer than five candidates, including O' Malley spoke in the halls and from hotel balconies of Queenstown alone. If Queenstown was important so was Zeehan and most of them moved there in the following week. All had advertised in the press, but none in the way that O' Malley did in the Zeehan and Dunhas Herald of March 11th inserted notice:

KING O' MALLEY

THE DEMOCRATIC CANDIDATE

for the Federal House of Representatives will

Talk Federation, Fossildom and the Bob-Tailed Boxers

ACADEMY   WEDNESDAY MARCH 13   8.P.M.

The Academy of Music was packed to hear the candidates, the audience including the usuals large content of ladies in whom he was always warmly received. O' Malley was intent on pressing home the point of a ' real democratic policy and one of justice', he proceeded to launch into a blistering attack on free trade and spoke from the heart of his own experience and was strong on the course of Old Age Pension to be carried by the Commonwealth and not be left to the whims of each State. He proceeds then to talk about free education... The great men of Tasmania had it an indefensible intellectual desert, because all true men of an ability sprang from the working class...]

O' Malley pointed out that [he wanted to regulate inter-state navigation...also a department of labor and a Ministerial portfolio, and compulsory arbitration and conciliation...a uniform patent law...an usury law....universal suffrage, and absentee tax... Federal Civil servants to have decent wages and Commonwealth police with commensurate pay. On the question of purchasing the site for a federal capital...he would take 60 per cent of the deposits of the banks, giving States notes in exchange...for the purpose of having money for the purchase of the territory. They could let the land on leases and gain substantial revenue. He would also have the Government take over the note issue and mint silver...if he headed the poll Barton had to give him a portfolio. If that was the case, then within two years he would have 200,000 pounds fro then purchase of lands for closer settlement.

CHAPTER 5.

A KING FOR REFORM

After a rowdy marathon speech with much interjections O' Malley sat down amid cheers. If it wasn't for his massive presence and public hearing he would not have got to first base with the masses. The press that once accepted his radical American views, his self promotional adverts in their newspapers, had suddenly turned against him as the election for the Tasmania representative in the new Federal Government drew closer. The Launceston *Examiner* referred to him as having 'a screw loose.' The *Zeehan and Dundas Herald* launched vicious attack on him in an effort to prevent his election, accusing him of representing capitalists interest and of doing nothing for his time on the Mainland but talk of being all things to all people. The newspaper editorial on O' Malley stated: [Canadian by birth, American by education, Australian by adoption, Irish through his father and English through his mother.]

The newspapers were relentless in their criticism of O' Malley and what would be the consequences if he won in the Tasmanian election. In the press it was considered 'He would make the miner, the labourer and the mechanic the prey of huge trust which was constantly being formed to throw down men of employment, to keep down wages and increase the price to the customer. He would have labouring classes of all grades placed under the heel of the plutocrat, who will grind out their life's blood…it will be a calamity to Tasmania and the whole of the Commonwealth if men like the candidate in question are sent to the Commonwealth Legislature.]

It was the fear of the conservative press of O' Malley not representing the people of Tasmania to the best advantage in parliament because he was a foreigner that was of issue. Then there was the view of him as a buffoon who would only lower the dignity of parliament and the esteem of Tasmania. But then the most important issue on their behalf was O' Malley's rigid protectionist views on tariffs "where the newspapers were overwhelmingly centred for free trade. Across Australia there was within the States an even balance between revenue tariff and protective tariff." This was the main concern of the Tasmanian newspapers and there made no pretence of being impartial in that regard. So they allowed large amounts of advertising space to those candidates who were more for free trade at the expense of O' Malley's efforts to get press coverage before the final days of the election. So it was of little surprise that Braddon won the vote in Launceston, be that only by a low margin.

As was expected supporters of O' Malley in the mining areas of Queenstown, Strahan and Zeehan polled him in the lead. The population at large were surprised to find that he had polled well in almost every area in the State. The victory celebration passed off quickly as O' Malley was already on his way to Melbourne to get ready for the opening of Parliament by the Duke of York. Once again he was member of Parliament, and was determined to be an outstanding feature. At the first opportunity he made his way to Parliament House in Melbourne and became the first member to mark out his seat on the back ministerial bench in readiness for his renewed vigour as the man of vision for the nation, and the peoples of Tasmania.

The Duke of Cornwall and York (later King George V) opened the first Commonwealth Parliament in Melbourne on 9 May, 1901. Thousands of people watched the royal procession as it made its way through the streets of the city to the Exhibition Building where the ceremony was witnessed by 12,000 invited guests.

The new century dawned on a cloudy Tuesday 1st January 1901 as the new nation simultaneously celebrated in Centennial Park, Sydney with a crowd over 700,000, the first Governor General Lord Hopetoun's inauguration of the Commonwealth of Australia. But it was not that event on New Years day- it was the opening of Parliament scheduled for May-that was to be the momentous occasion. It is unknown if O' Malley was in Sydney for the GG's inauguration, but he was on May 9th at the opening of the 1st Parliament in the splendorous great Exhibition building in Melbourne by the Duke of Cornwall and York. No fewer than 10,000 people were crowded into that building that day, when the Duke declared parliament opened. O' Malley took pride of place immediately in front of the dais with fellow members. Like all his fellow elected members of the new parliament, O'Malley heard the Duke read a message from the King and was then sworn in. The would-a-be British subject had overcome his former conscientious objection status and was sworn in. The election of the Speaker of the House followed and to O' Malley's delight resulted in the position going to Frederick Holder, his old acquaintance from the House of Assembly in Adelaide.

The Assembly house was led by new PM Edmond Barton, with Alfred Deakin as Attorney General, and on the front benchWilliam Lyne for Home Affairs from New South Wales, George Turner from Victoria as Treasurer, Charles Cameron Kingston from South Australia for Trade and Customs, James Duke from Queensland as Postmaster General, Richard Edward O' Connor, QC, from New South Wales as Vice-President and two term serving Tasmanian Premier Philip Oakley Fysh without portfolio. Not forgetting the famous John Forrest explorer, who at the age of 22, on his first expedition undertaken in 1869, mainly to find the remains of Leichhardt, he travelled over 2,000 miles in the interior of Western Australia. He discovered and named Lake Barlee, and Mount Ida, Leonora, Malcolm and Margaret. Forrest for WA was given Defence. All the seats were represented more or less on an equal physical status, if not so much on an intellectual level. And on the back bench the most outlandish independent of all- King O' Malley who would offend extremes of intellectual genius and blundering clownery prove to be a thorn in the side of the many on the front bench for the next two decades.

It is worthy to comment on those members elected to the front bench as the first representatives of our Australian new federal government, for their contribution of a wealth life experience in their prior entry to parliament and beyond, shaped our nation to be second to none both domestically and in the international arena. But it is also fitting to delve into the character and abilities of these politicians to view from afar the floor of that early parliament and what O' Malley's ego, street wise debating skills and dogged will was to contend with.

Edmund Barton as first Prime Minister was certainly qualified for his new job. He had been a member of the Parliament of New South Wales for 20 years, and had served terms as Speaker of its Legislative Assembly, Attorney-General and Leader of the Opposition. He became a barrister in 1871 and set up a successful legal practice, joining the Sydney Mechanics Institute to learn the art of debating which led him to politics. An omnivorous reader he loved the theatre—especially Shakespeare and the opera—and appreciated music and art. He was the ideal choice at the time to be our First Prime Minister.

Alfred Deakin was politician, statesman and barrister who served as the second Prime Minister of Australia, who was to serve from 1903 to 1904, 1905 to 1908 and 1909 to 1910, holding office as the leader of the Protectionist Party, and in his final term as leader of the Liberal Party. Deakin was Australia's second prime minister. Deakin was a lawyer who had another string to his bow – journalism. He wrote anonymous newspaper articles about federal politics for many years even while Prime Minister. His government introduced tariff protection and old age pensions.

William Lyle was a tall, tough countryman from southern New South Wales, not very smart, but determined. In politics he represented the selectors in his district. He became the leader of the Protectionist Party, which wanted to help selectors by keeping cheaper wheat from other colonies out of New South Wales. In the 1890s he was the leader of the opposition to George Reid's free-trade government, which was supported by the new Labor Party. Lyne persuaded Labor to switch support to him by offering to pass more laws to help workers. So he became premier in 1899, just before Federation. He himself had opposed Federation because he thought the small states should not have the same number of senators as the large. John Hopetoun, the Governor-General, chose him to be the first Prime Minister because he was premier of the oldest colony. Edmund Barton, Alfred Deakin and other protectionists refused to be ministers under a man who had opposed the cause they had worked so hard for. Lyne then recommended to the governor-general that he appoint Barton as prime minister. Barton in return made him a minister in his government.

In 1894 George Turner became Victoria's first Australian-born premier inheriting a state suffering from severe economic depression. He was also treasurer. Victoria had made a fortunate choice, for other radicals such as Isaac Isaacs (later the first Australian-born Governor- General), Turner set about restoring Victoria to financial health. He slashed costs, introduced a graduated income tax, reformed bankruptcy laws and established the State Savings Bank. He won two more state elections before resigning to join federal politics.

Charles Kingston, was a big, imposing man with full beard, booming voice with a cutting debating style, who dominated the small world of South Australian politics in the 1890s as a radical liberal party leader. Kingston was a dominant and outstanding figure in late colonial politics in South Australia and one of the leading-figures in bringing about the establishment of the federal government. He was a strong advocate of a white Australia policy an opponent of Chinese immigration,and had much to do with framing the formula for its regulation. Federal Labor parliamentarians later described him as the originator of the White Australia policy. In His State Government ministry Kingston was popularly credited with extension of the franchise to women, establishment of a state bank, a high protective tariff, regulation of factories, and a progressive system of land and income taxation. He is still regarded in radical circles as one of the greatest Australians, a tremendous reformer, and a wild man to boot. However, he was also an autocrat with a titanic ego, and the passions which often motivated him were not those of a gentle idealist. Deakin, admired his 'great ability' and 'indomitable will', noted that 'No man more enjoyed the confidence of the masses'. Beatrice Webb had mixed feelings when she met him in 1898. She admired him as 'an industrious, upright and capable administrator, with great Parliamentary powers'. At the same time she was disturbed by his 'spite' and 'demagogic dislike of any distinction or superiority.'

John Forrest from Western Australia I have already mentioned. More than any other Australian politician, John Forrest was the leader of his colony. He was born in it, had explored it and became its first premier in 1890. He was a big man, not very clever, but honest, good at his job and a great believer in Western Australia. He was a conservative who supported many changes so that his colony could become more advanced like the rest. Forrest supported Federation, but was worried that his colony would suffer when the duties on goods from the eastern colonies had to be removed. Many of his supporters from the old farming areas were totally opposed to Federation. The diggers on the new goldfields, already unhappy with Forrest's rule, wanted Federation. They said if Forrest did not let them vote on it, they would separate from Western Australia and join Australia. Forrest had got some special terms for his colony, and when it was clear that he could not get any more, he did allow a vote on Federation. The colony voted 'Yes'. Forrest was elected to the Commonwealth Parliament and became minister of defence in the Edmund Barton's government.

James Drake former Jackaroo, Journalist and Lawyer, and military man as Major in the Queensland defence force, was a member of the legislative of Assembly of Queensland for the district of Enoggera from th May 1888 to 7th December 1899. Following his years of service he was appointed a life Member of the legislative Council of Queensland and on 7 December 1899, he was appointed Postmaster-General and Secretary for Public Instruction in Queensland. Although membership of the Legislative Council was a life appointment, he resigned on 13 May 1901 in order to pursue a career in newly established federal parliament After federation on 1 January 1901, Edmond Barton formed a caretaker ministry with James Dickson as Queensland's sole representative. Dickson's sudden death just over a week later caused Barton to seek another Queenslander to join his ministry. Drake was offered the position, and as a result he was appointed Post-Master General on 5 February 1901.

He was elected to the Senate as a Protectionist at the inaugural federal election held the following month. Drake was tasked with establishing a national post and telegraph system from the six existing colonial systems. He secured the passage of the *Post and Telegraph Act 1901*, in his second reading speech expressing the need for non-discrimination in the provision of services and the advantages of a publicly owned telegraph service. He was generally regarded as a competent administrator, but a plodder – thorough rather than brilliant." He subsequently held ministerial office under prime ministers Barton, Deakin and Reid, serving as Post Master General (1901–1903), Minister for Defence (1903), Attorney-General (1903–1904), and Vice President of the Executive Council (1904–1905).

Philips Fysh, tall and willowy, was an impressive figure with his flowing white beard. Always a private man, he left very little of a personal nature on record. His keen sense of public responsibility, however, is shown in his involvement with numerous community organisations. Appointed justice of the peace in 1867, he was a city alderman in 1868-69, with the establishment of the Commonwealth, entered Federal politics as minister without portfolio in 1901-03, and postmaster-general in

1903-04, and later president of the Central Board of Health and chairman of the Metropolitan Drainage Board. Co-founder and sometime president of the Hobart Working Men's Club, he also supported the Ragged Schools Association, the Ccouncil of Hobart High School, the Hobart Benevolent Society and the Tasmanian Political Reform Association. He held the rank of major in the Tasmanian Volunteer Rifle Regiment. He was appointed K.C.M.G. in 1896, an honour he had declined in 1891; he received an honorary Oxford D.C.L. in 1901. As member for Denison during the last years of his political career he was forced into the role of a conservative in response to the growing influence of the Labor Party, whose creed he abhorred. He retired from politics in 1910 and farmed in the Derwent Valley.

Richard Edward (Dick) O'Connor (1851-1912),Barrister, Federationist and Judge, claimed to be descent from Arthur O'Connor, Irish rebel and a general in Napoleon's army. In 1874 he began to study law. O'Connor was admitted to the Bar on 15 June 1876. He 'devilled' for Darley for two years and eked out his income by contributing to the Echo, Freeman's Journal and Evening News, and by law reporting. After five years in the Volunteer Artillery, Sergeant O'Connor received the customary land order, sold the land and started his magnificent law library. In 1878-83 he was crown prosecutor for the northern district and built up a successful practice, mainly in common law and in Banco, from his chambers in Wentworth Court. Although an avowed protectionist, O'Connor was nominated to the Legislative Council on 30 December 1887 on Sir Henry Parkes's recommendation. On 23 October 1891 he became minister for justice, with the right of private practice, in George Dib's protectionist cabinet; from July to September 1893 he was also solicitor-general. When Barton was Attorney-General O'Connor carried important legislation to amend the law relating to joint-stock companies, trade marks, marriage, lunacy and summary convictions, and to improve procedure in the Probate Court. Night after night he piloted through committee the complex Parliamentary Electorates and Elections Act of 1893 and was repeatedly frustrated in his efforts to introduce the draft Constitution bill.

Before taking office O'Connor and Barton had accepted briefs for the plaintiff in Proudfoot vs the Railway Commissioners (who retained their own solicitor). The case dragged on and in November 1893 the propriety of ministers of the Crown acting against a government department (albeit a statutory authority) was questioned in Parliament. They immediately relinquished their briefs and, after a motion was carried against them in the assembly on 7th December, resigned their portfolios. O'Connor, mentally and physically exhausted, went overseas in 1894 to recuperate and visited Egypt, Italy, England and Ireland. In Rome he 'met some very fine old Priests & Bishops ... men of strong intellect, wide knowledge, full of toleration & sympathy for everything', whom he wished Dibbs could meet. Returning invigorated, in 1895 O'Connor successfully defended William Crick on conspiracy charges arising out of the Dean case. He took silk in 1896 and was engaged as counsel for the plaintiff in McSharry v the Railway Commissioners, another protracted suit over disputed costs. From November 1898 to March 1899 he was an acting Supreme Court judge.

Well rather than widely read and a Shakespeare lover, O'Connor belonged to the Athenaeum Club in its heyday and to the Australian Club from 1890. He was a fellow of St John's College in 1874-87 and of the university senate in 1890-91 and 1893-1912. Tall, with a trim beard and luxuriant moustache, he was seen by Alfred Deakin as 'one of the type of the Spanish Irish, dark of complexion, regular of feature, the head somewhat small for the upright, well-set, deep-chested, vigorous frame'. George Cockerill found him 'somewhat grim-visaged, but possessing a ready smile that illumined his countenance'. O'Connor was no great orator, but 'his conversational voice was rich and musical, and his personal magnetism was such as to disarm opposition'.

From 1889 O'Connor and Barton had been 'comrades in the struggle for union'. They were founders of the Australasian Federation League of New South Wales in 1893 and of the Central Federation League in 1896. O'Connor addressed many meetings and that year was a delegate to the People's Federal Convention at Bathurst. In 1897 he was elected to the Australasian Federal Convention. Like Barton, he was familiar with the American, Canadian and Swiss Constitutions and had made a special study of constitutional law. When the convention met in Adelaide O'Connor was elected to the constitutional and drafting committees, although almost completely unknown outside New South Wales. He did his best work 'by patient listening to others', and by helping Barton to reconcile 'the views of the Convention into one harmonious whole'. He also did 'a lot of work for which Toby Barton gets the credit'.

After unsuccessfully campaigning throughout the colony for the draft Constitution bill's acceptance, O'Connor resigned from the Legislative Council in July 1898 to contest the assembly seat of Young. Fighting on Federation issues, he was naively surprised to find himself confronted by 'country unions' and was defeated by Chris Watson. Piqued, he confided to Deakin, now a close friend, 'I don't like the idea of being licked in my first attempt to enter the Assembly'. In 1899 he campaigned less actively for the second Constitution bill referendum as he realised that he 'had to stick to my business as it began to come back or I would have been in a disastrous plight'. He still managed to speak 'four or five nights a week' in Sydney. When in December 1900 the Governor-General, Lord Hopetoun, commissioned Sir William Lyne instead of Barton to form the first Commonwealth ministry, O'Connor refused to serve under Lyne and was active in the behind-the-scenes negotiations that led him to resign his commission. Barton announced his cabinet on Christmas Day: O'Connor was vice-president of the Executive Council (an honorary portfolio). In March 1901 he was elected to the Senate at the top of the poll-the only Protectionist Senator returned for New South Wales.

As government leader O'Connor displayed hitherto unsuspected parliamentary dexterity in managing the hostile Senate through three very stormy sessions, without incurring any major defeats. In Cabinet, he was sagacious, wise, and far-seeing. In the House he was uniformly calm, courteous and courageous, and was 'the best-liked man' in parliament. O'Connor's greatest achievement was steering the 1902 Customs Tariff Act through the Senate virtually unaltered, after ceaseless conflict & hard work'. Next year, when the Lower House refused to accept a Senate amendment to the sugar bounty bill that in effect increased taxation, he persuaded the Senate not to insist. From the opening of parliament he was responsible for discouraging the Senate from voting as a States' house and convinced the majority that it was their duty to bow to the wishes of the House of Representatives. He was one of the few whose reputation was 'enhanced by Federation'. His control was the more remarkable as he struggled to maintain his practice in Sydney between parliamentary sessions in Melbourne, but found there was no longer 'the same continuous stream that used to make my business so good'. The Catholic Press believed he had sacrificed an income of £4000 a year to accept office. In June 1901 he reluctantly told Deakin that he could not continue without some remuneration; Sir John Forrest agreed that it was 'unreasonable' to expect him too 'do ministerial work for nothing'. As the number of salaried ministers was limited by the Constitution, each consented to contribute £200 a year to a fund for honorary ministers. Connor's last major task in the Senate was to carry the Judiciary Act of 1903 establishing the High Court of Australia.

So thus we have insight into character for such men of noble duty who were the makers of political argument and policy during the early days of Federal Government. O' Malley was too content with the highest of intellect and those nor so intelligent but honest. There lay the ground swell of the normal stand of human decency, and dignity was often tested in the field of debate over matters of importance and the not so for the benefit of all in our nation. Whilst there were moments of brilliant perception by O' Malley, engrained in him over his former lifetime as insurance salesman, real estate , gold speculator and not the least member of State parliament, he was subjected to the high winds of oratory that tested his spiritual values and political mission as member of parliament. It was this character of O'Malley, his historic hard won battles, flamboyancy, mode of dress and way with words that would forge in him a fire burning brightly for the nation from the very first day of his post until its very last two decades later. But back to the progress but not perfection of this man of many appearances.

Of course, this is not about me and my moral compass as to the fact that O' Malley was there at the beginning of Federation, and the introduction of the Lord prayer in the House was no doubt recited by him on every attendance. It seems from O' Malley's lips on past occasions he had stated he had some influence by religious teaching in his early life most probably through his Irish ancestry, but fell out with the teachings of all religions and was for every more an opponent of its doctrines of faith and morals.

Born in the frontier regions of the wild west of the time church count-
ed for little. So it is doubtful if O' Malley ever acquired a deep feeling
or need for a moral compass of the conventional religions. There was a
time he had declared that his parents were Presbyterian from Northern
Ireland and had little or no regard for the Catholic Church. But little
reliance can be placed on his statements about his parentage. In the December 1896 a libel case he brought against William Moorhead he has
stated that he said he was an American. "…that he had been brought up
as a Catholic, been converted to Wesley'd view of faith and morals, but
removed it all on the shoulder of two asses because of doubts as to the
sincerity of his conversion."

O' Malley was in many ways an enigma. He proclaimed to be of Canadian birth but promoted not so much British values as would seem to be
the custom for a Commonwealth Government representative but boast-
ed and promoted all things American. He strongly supported the federation of Australia in parliamentary speeches but championed the U.S.
constitution as the best model. He was a convert to the early Methodist
and a propagandist against alcohol, a 'land boomer' and insurance man
with, at best, a flexible code of ethics. O'Malley lived by his own version of religious morals in all his dealing throughout his life inside an
outside of politics and in his own way had no wish to change that which
he believed to be right for him. It seems in O' Malley's eyes he was a
moral and religious man, but his morality and religion, which were as
patronal to him, were as outlandish as his flamboyant dress and eccentric speech.

The Court case against Moorhead is an important episode in King O'
Malley's life in Australia because it laid clear for all who wished to see
the probable outline of his life before coming to Australia. At the time
O' Malley refused to go into the witness box to be cross examined on
his former religious upbringing nor make any further statement as
such.. Born and raised in the Kansas of the wild west, he had extensive
travels on the frontiers of the Pacific Coast in time and place where religious belief was not a priority to those early adventurous the likes of
the King of Insurance and real estate deals. As a staunch Republican O'
Malley 'stumped' the midwest in support of candidate James Blaine for
president in the 1884 campaign. Blain was supported enthusiastically
by his followers ,despite financial scandals, appeared to have a good

chance of winning. In an election marked by reversals of fortune and outright ballot- rigging, Grover Cleveland the democratic candidate triumphs by a mere 23,005 votes and O' Malley's hopes were dashed. Years later he recalled: "I did for Blaine in 1884 and had he gone all the way I would have been ambassador to Chilli."

On 7th June 1901 the House of Representatives agreed to a motion 'That the Standing Orders should provide that, upon Mr Speaker taking the Chair, he shall read a prayer'. An amendment providing for the appointment of a chaplain for the purpose was withdrawn, as it was agreed that the Speaker was the most appropriate person to read prayers in the House.The Speaker then reads the following prayers **"Almighty God, we humbly beseech Thee to vouch safe Thy blessing upon this Parliament. Direct and prosper our deliberations to the advancement of Thy glory, and the true welfare of the people of Australia."**
And all the members of parliament responded with the Lord's prayer: "Our Father, which art in Heaven: Hallowed be Thy Name. Thy Kingdom come. Thy will be done in earth, as it is in Heaven. Give us this day our daily bread. And forgive us our trespasses, as we forgive them that trespass against us. And lead us not into temptation; but deliver us from evil: For Thine is the kingdom, and the power, and the glory, for ever and ever. Amen."

I have always taken note that the Lord's prayer is spoken before the House of Representative before waffling in debate the for and against motions, that if carried go to the Senate for approval. Interestingly though The Lord's prayer recited in Parliament has one erroneous word that leans to a different meaning than the prayer recited in Christian Churches to this very day. It is the world 'in- thy will be done in earth and not on earth as it was reportedly recited my Christ and written in the New Testament. For the word in earth is the home of death and darkness where as on earth is the place of the living humanity. A moot point I agree but the floors of Parliament is a home of ravenous wolves and logical linear minds and not much there that speaks of "Gods will be done" I dare to state herein.

O' Malley, despite constant interjections to the standing orders did not-involve himself in the debate of that day but instead chose the time to make his maiden speech- on the unlikely topic of the need or not of prayers being read when the Speaker took the chair. Knox, the member of the wealth electorate of Koonyong, himself a pillar of the Presbyterian Church, moved the motion 'that standing orders should provide that, upon Mr Speaker taking the chair he shall read a prayer' and declared that the Anglican, Presbyterian, Methodist, Congregational and Baptist churches all desired that it should be done. Glenn, as a Roman Catholic, seconded the motion, suggesting a form the Lord's prayer in the revised version with the hope that..'we may possibly take from its spirit, and the feeling of ultimate aim induced by its repetition in common, a larger measure of charity and mutual toleration'.

In support of the motion O' Malley moved an amendment to the effect that the prayer should be said by a chaplain appointed for that purpose. He was devout and he said:...'I am a man of then world and I have had a lot of experience' and then went on, much to the Speaker's displeasure to refer to the loss a few years previously of the mace from the Victorian Houses of Parliament and he remembered ' ... that the mace became one of the objects of ridicule of one of Solomon's lilies in this city.' The point of his remark- that the Speaker at some future time might be a good man and it might not be inappropriate for him to say prayers-was largely lost on the House and was certainly not taken seriously by the press which, instead, devoted much cartoon space to picture O' Malley and Sir Matthew Davies looking for the mace among 'Solomon's lilies' in Melbourne. The amendment was withdrawn and it was pointed out that a chaplain acceptable to all religions was unlikely, and the Lords prayer read by then Speaker of the House and recited by parliamentary representative before debate was then written into standing orders and still remains.

In the earliest of debates it was declared that a revenue and protective tariff would be introduced, an investigation into the railway border control dispute between Western Australian and South Australian border be considered to be surrendered to The Northern Territory, and that the defences of the Commonwealth be strengthened as well as a uniform postage be introduced. The deferment of the old age pension must have displeased O' Malley but the promise of action on banking, immigration and the promise of federal capital gave him plenty to consider.

William Morris Hughes, who later became the second longest serving Prime Minister in Australian politics, was a thorn in the side for O'Malley from the first day they each attended parliament. They in many opposing views of matters of the debate and personal vindictiveness were not hidden to the fellow members of the house of parliament. Their prolonged and bitter feud lasted for decades. Hughes' life prior to entering parliament and upbringing may well have been an influence on his attitude towards O' Malley. His father was Welsh speaking, a deacon of the particular Baptist Church and a conservative in politics. His mother had died when he was seven and for the next five years Hughes lived with his father's sister at Llandudno, where he went to school, spending his holidays on the Morris farm. A lively youth, fonder of games than of lessons, he won a prize for French and caught the eye of the inspector, Matthew Arnold. He remained as an assistant after his five years apprenticeship, and joined a volunteer battalion of the Royal Fusiliers nearby. Why Hughes decided to migrate is unknown. Long hours in ill-ventilated and overcrowded classrooms had probably affected his health, and his deafness may already have begun.

In October 1884 he embarked for Queensland and for two years led a roving life, then as a galley-hand on a coastal boat, he arrived at Sydney. After a period of acute poverty he found a steady job as assistant to an oven-maker and domestic stability in a boarding-house near Moore Park. In 1890 he married and moved to Balmain where he opened a small mixed shop, took on odd jobs and mended umbrellas. Hughes's shop sold political pamphlets, and the back room became a meeting-place for young reformers. The visit to Sydney that year of Henry George stirred his imagination and Hughes made his political début as a street-corner speaker for the Balmain Single Tax League. His electioneering in the harbour-side city seat was enlivened by his and his friends' production of a weekly newspaper, the New Order; when he won by 105 votes he was drawn in triumph through the city in a dog-cart, his supporters having first bought him a decent suit.

In parliament he proved a shrewd tactician and effective speaker. He could win over the rowdiest meeting and any attempt to step out of line in his absence was quelled on his return. As a sideline, he organised the Trolley, Draymen and Carters' Union and became its president. He took advantage of the Federal parliament's location in Melbourne to organise the Waterside Workers' Federation; the executive was recruited from the members of parliament for the various ports, and again Hughes was president. He passed the bar as a lawyer in 1905, was chairman of the royal commission on navigation (1904-07), became familiar with conditions on the ships as well as on the wharves, and made useful contacts with other maritime unions. Hughes, was an unusual creature in the House-a labor member and a convinced free-trader. O'Malley was an independent with labor leanings but held strong protectionist leanings. Hughes in the earliest of debates declared the government lacked courage in not bringing tariff in line with its views and that present tariff gave an unfair advantage to a section of the community at the expense of the whole community.

This was too much for O' Malley who interjected frequently in opposition to Hughes. The discussion degenerated into an argument with Hughes statements flatly denied by O'Malley until Hughes attempted to crush O'Malley with the statement:-'It is lamentable thing that my honourable friend was not coeval with the creator at the making of the universe, because I feel convinced that he would have given Him a great many hints. I particularly regret that my honourable friend was not a member of the Convention that framed the Constitution, and it is much more to be regretted that it is only our descendants who-come after us who will feel the great loss then unsustained through the honourable members absence.' To this O' Malley simply replied 'The honourable member is quite right.' and ignored the chance to speak on the rest of the the debate.

O' Malley, apart from his on going doused with William Morris Hughes over numerous matters in Parliament for the betterment of the Australian people knew that he needed to devote more time to matters concerning his constituents., particularly those who had voted him in on his cause for the temperance movement in Tasmania and the rights of women. But it was more than that, it was a badge of honour for him not being a drinker, that he wore with pride, and he so often wove his ideas in the importance of sobriety into his parliamentary speeches. It was too this cause he later worked tirelessly to see the banning of Alcohol in the new capital of Canberra that lasted from 1911 to 1928 in his final term in office.

Temperance societies proliferated after the 1832 arrival of the Quakers, James Backhouse and George Washington Walker in Tasmania, who started a pledge to abstain from alcoholic beverages. In 1836 the Tasmanian Temperance Society took the teetotal pledge, while the moderate Launceston Temperance Society only opposed excessive drinking.

Temperance was a key issue of the 1850s in a colony where convicts lowered the tone of society, liquor consumption was heavy, and there was widespread poverty and drunkenness, few women to exert a moderating influence and limited entertainment alternatives. Publicans were the largest commercial group on the island, with an estimation of one public house to every 127 inhabitants. Temperance advocates saw alcohol as the source of society's degeneration, affecting the 'health, temporal prosperity, domestic comfort, and moral and religious well-being of man' as well as being closely linked to crime. The start of the decade saw overlapping membership in movements to upgrade society, through anti- transportation and temperance. Temperance activities, primarily by middle-class evangelical Christians, were largely directed towards the working class. To counter the public-house, recreational facilities were established: coffee houses, temperance hotels, debating clubs, reading rooms, youth organisations and festivals. Brass bands were popular, with enthusiastic and vocal audiences at temperance meetings.

During the 1850s the total abstainers gained ascendancy and were almost successful in their appeals for a dry colony similar to Maine, USA – presenting five parliamentary petitions containing over 10,000 signatures. The powerful liquor industry opposed prohibitory legislation; economically, the government derived 55 percent of its revenue from the duties placed on spirits.. Bitter controversy over the Sunday closing of public-houses saw leading temperance advocate 'Coffee Pot' Crouch and others publicly threatened with tar and feathering in 1855 for organising a vigilante group to enforce Sunday closure. Part of an international organisation that traced the major defects and evils in society to alcohol abuse, the Women's Christian Temperance Union was active in Tasmania between 1885 and 1914, believing the moral superiority of women gave them the responsibility to uplift the morality and purity of all Tasmanians, and actively pursued temperance through petitions. education, local option, the suffrage movement and public awareness.

CHAPTER 6.

THE TEETOTALLER

O' Malley in his canvassing was always capitalist on temperance movement in Tasmania and gained many supporters to his cause of the dangers of 'stagger juice.'

To get it as to why King O' Malley was so publicly anti what he called ' Stagger juice', we have to go back to the beginning of alcohol and its effects on Americans from its beginnings where he obviously witnessed so much alcohol abuse, sickness and disease as a result of its consumption during his frontier existence in his younger days in America. A number of factors led to an explosion of alcohol consumption in the early 1800s there. First, the British halted the participation in the American molasses/rum trade, objecting to its connections with slavery, while the federal government also began to tax rum in the 1790s.

[At the same time, the settlement of the so-called "corn belt" in the Midwest created large new supplies of corn, which was much cheaper and more profitable to convert into whiskey than it was to transport great distances without spoiling. Thus, it was noted that "Western farmers could make no profit shipping corn overland to eastern markets, so they distilled corn into 'liquid assets.' By the 1820s, whiskey sold for twenty-five cents a gallon, making it cheaper than beer, wine, coffee, tea, or milk."]

In short, whiskey was extremely cheap and extremely available, and American consumption soared as a result. As Daniel Okrent describes in *Last Call*, the number of distilleries in the nation increased fivefold, to 14,000 in between 1790 and 1810. He writes that "in cities it was widely understood that common workers would fail to come to work on Mondays, staying home to wrestle with the echoes and aftershocks of a weekend binge. By 1830, the tolling of a town bell at 11 a.m. and again at 4 p.m. marked 'grog time."

Back then so much of this drinking was actually being done by the upper class, including the great political statesmen of the day. Author Daniel Okrent, in his book Last Call: The Rise and fall of Prohibition, notes one particularly raucous political function: "George Clinton, governor of New York from 1777 to 1795, once honoured the French ambassador with a dinner for 120 guests, who together drank '135 bottles of madeira, 36 bottles of port, 60 bottles of English beer and 30 large cups of rum punch."

Likewise, most of the founding fathers enjoyed hitting the bottle, and doing it hard. From Okrent's book: [Washington kept a still on his farm, John Adams began each day with a tankard of hard cider, and Thomas Jefferson's fondness for drink extended beyond his renowned collection of wines to encompass rye whiskey made from his own crops. James Madison consumed a pint of whiskey daily. Soldiers in the U.S. Army had been receiving four ounces of whiskey as part of their daily ration since 1782; George Washington himself said 'the benefits arising from moderate use of strong liquor have been experienced in all armies, and are not to be disputed.']

Before European colonisation, the native population of the territory that would eventually become the United States was relatively naïve to alcohol's effects. Some tribes produced weak beers or other fermented beverages, but these were generally used only for ceremonial purposes. The distillation of more potent and thus more abusable forms of alcohol was unknown. When various European colonists suddenly made large amounts of distilled spirits and wine available to American Indians, the tribes had little time to develop social, legal, or moral guidelines to regulate alcohol use. Early traders quickly established a demand for alcohol by introducing it as a medium of trade, often using it in exchange for highly sought-after animal skins and other resources. Traders also found that providing free alcohol during trading sessions gave them a distinct advantage in their negotiations.

Extreme intoxication was common among the colonists and provided a powerful model for the social use of alcohol among the inexperienced Indian populations. Numerous historical accounts describe extremely violent bouts of drinking among Indian tribes during trading sessions and on other occasions, but at least as many accounts exist of similar behaviour among the colonising traders, military personnel, and civilians (Smart and Osborne 1996). Such modelling was not limited to the early colonial era but continued as the land was colonised from East to West; trappers, miners, soldiers, and lumbermen were well known for their heavy drinking sprees.

History may have therefore sown the seeds for the prevalence of alcohol abuse in North American indigenous populations. Early demand, with no regulation and strong encouragement, may have contributed to a "tradition" of heavy alcohol use passed down from generation to generation, which has led to the current high level of alcohol-related problems.

Whilst Alcohol and the abuse of it was mainly in the Elite classes of Americans early colonial years it soon spread across the nation to native Americans as pioneers moved west. The consequences of alcohol abuse for Native Americans include increased risks of heart disease, cancer, gastrointestinal problems, pneumonia, tuberculosis, dental problems, hearing and vision problems, depression, and other mental health disorders. King O' Malley must have seen much of this in his days of blazing his trail as an insurance salesman and land dealer from the east to the west of the Americas of his day.

In the making of illicit whiskey from corn crops called Moonshine, is high-proof liquor, generally whiskey, was traditionally made, or at least distributed, illegally. Its clandestine distribution is known as bootlegging. The name was derived from a tradition of creating the alcohol during the night time, thereby avoiding detection.. The taxing of liquors and spirits was an effective way to generate revenue for the government. In the early frontier days of American history, moonshine wasn't a hobby: it was a part-time job. Many farmers relied on "moonshine" manufacturing to survive in bad years on the land. Low-value corn crops could be turned into high-value whisky. Farmer-distillers in the western part of the state protested when the federal government passed the distilled-spirits tax in 1791. They tarred and feathered tax collectors and fired upon their homes.

History, by and large, tends to be considerably more complicated than our pop cultural understanding of it. A historical movement as broad as the prohibition of alcohol in the United States, for instance, was the result of so much more than a mere crusade of moralistic teetotallers. Just as it's grossly, hilariously simplistic to describe a conflict such as the Civil War as having been fought "to end slavery," it's equally myopic to think about a topic as complex as Prohibition in the terms of "drinkers vs non-drinkers." In reality, there were so many other racial, political, religious, economic and nationalistic factors in play that the full story is actually an unlikely coming-together of many groups with very disparate goals, held in a bizarre alliance by their opposition to the alcohol industry.

With all of that said, though, there's one aspect of the road to Prohibition that is undeniable, and that's the American appetite for alcohol. In short: It has always been a nation of drunks, but by today's standards, average alcohol consumption in large parts of the 19th century U.S.A. was almost beyond rational belief. You will likely find it hard to accept as a fact just how much booze the average American was consuming in the 1800's.

When he first arrived in Australia, O'Malley reported that he started the Waterlily Rockbound Church – the Redskin Church of the Cayuse Nation, Texas in the US, where he was its first and only (self-elected) bishop. It was at that time he converted to following the temperance movement. He disliked alcohol, calling it 'stagger juice'. O'Malley was interested in social issues and the rights of women. In that he saw much abuse in the hotels of the shanty towns he visited in his travels. Even with his temperance views, he lobbied for the law to ensure that barmaids be treated with respect because "innocent girls are back slapped and monkeyed with".

O' Malley swore and declared he had always been a teetotaller all his life in his early days in Australia and continued to preach the same in his oratory in Tasmania, South Australia and Victoria, especially when he was canvassing life insurance in and around the hotels or for a seat in both State and the new federal governments at the turn of the 20th century. There was only one ever press article that gave reference to O' Malley having been sited in Hobart during a canvassing expedition for the sale of life insurance. It was reported that he was seen in a state of inebriation in a Hobart pub in the company off two prostitutes. O' Malley came out with guns blazing at the paper, journalist and the scoundrel who perpetrated the lie to blacken his good name. He demanded a retraction and apology by the press and offered to hang draw and quarter or more severely disembowel the culprit who spread the rumour if he had the opportunity. Further, he stated that he never ever drank alcohol, had no need of ladies of the night, and at the time of the alleged sight of him, he was in the company of friends at a Melbourne event and if necessary could prove same.

O'Malley claimed alcohol had a depressing influence and said, "stagger-juice and efficient public business are absolutely incompatible". So, in 1911 O'Malley triggered a type of prohibition that was to continue until 1928. This was the very first ordinance passed in the new federal capital territory. Unlike the US-style prohibition, the laws only prevented the granting of liquor licences. Locals could still bring alcohol into the territory and drink it there. One anomaly was the Cricketers' Arms Hotel (running from the 1860s until 1918). It was the Territory's only pub and was already operating, so it got around the rules. An irony, too, was that alcohol flowed freely at the naming of the city in 1913, and King O'Malley was a key participant in the formal proceedings. O'Malley's efforts "that the Territory shall be dry" did not quite succeed as he had hoped.

O' Malley in his retirement years must have been pleased to hear of the progress made in America when Bill Wilson, a stockbroker and Dr. Bob Smith formed Alcholics Anonymous in 1937. They had published the 'Big book,' on recovery in 1939, when their membership was about one hundred and had grown substantially at the time of O' Malley's death in 1953.

Whilst some members of the House and outsiders considered him a buffoon, he became well known to a wide group of the public. The press to a great degree could never make up their mind about O'Malley, The Melbourne Punch taking hold of the tariff incident on 13th June solemnly pronounced ['King O Malley stock has fallen to zero. Every parliament has its member pour wine. This is O' Malley's role.'] The Sydney Bulletin in its 15th June edition was more discerning and pronounced: [So far, the Commonwealth Parliament has discovered its clown…an attempt was made to fasten the office on King O' Malley- the big hat and spread-eagle ways enticed the unwary-but they found that they were trying to appoint a bull-ant to a performing sheep's billet and dropped the O'M in haste.]

Even the Age had declared: [King Edward is a much simpler and less affected man than King O' Malley…a poseur every waking moment of his life, theatrical to his finger tips, in bothy speech and dress, a weak imitator of the spread-eagle orators of the United States, he is the embodiment of vulgar display, and yet he thinks or professes to think that he is the most refined of enlightened democracy. It is certainly not much of recommendation for democracy.]

The Argus, who advocated violently for free trade, and at enmity with O' Malley throughout his parliamentary life, attacked him saying: [Mr O' Malley has been rapidly acquiring the well deserved position of a political nonentity. The House has almost ceased to laugh at his theatrical extravagances in dress and language and has commenced to regard his constant " hee-yur hee - yur" as a nuisance…the wild and whirling style of spread-eagle oratory…is not acceptable to it.]

Normally O' Malley did not react to press criticism philosophically but the Argus in particular infuriated him. so early in August in the House of Representatives, he declared [Some anthropological professor would say that the Argus was a sort of petrified corpse of Conservatism but I don't. I simply say it is an embalmed relic, or embodiment, of Conservative, antediluvian, fossilised mummydom masquerading in the pious garb of up-to-date hypocrisy.]

O'Malley soon acquired popular notoriety and was sometimes called ' the untamed terror of Tasmania.' Punch pointed out that when he was at Flemington racecourse he was pointed out to one visitor who exclaimed; 'Dear me, he is quite white?' 'What did you expect?' said his host. The visitor replied: 'Well 'v read many paragraphs about him, but I always thought that, like King Billy of Ballarat, King O' Malley was an Aboriginal from Mallee district."

Senator O' Keefe, also from Tasmania, in that same month as O' Malley threw in his lot with the Labor party because they were of similar agreement with the party values. It is uncertain how William Morris (Billy) Hughes felt about this move of O' Malley as he personally did not see in him a true representative of the working class in the well-to do 'American'. Hughes reflected in part his views in the *Worker*, published in Sydney, when asked about Senator O' Keefe and O' Malley joining the labor party:'… but neither of them can claim to know where the boot really punches the worker. However, their zeal to serve may make amends for their shortcomings afterwards.

 Looking forward in the vain of Hughes, is the gratitude of succeeding generations as O'Malley's claim in the part he played in the establishment of Canberra. Even before federation he displayed a keen interest in a location in the land tenure system of a national capital and it was sitting that on Friday 19th, 1901 he moved:[That, in the opinion of this House, it is desirable in the interest of human progress, that the Government secure as federal territory an area of land of not less than 1000 square miles in a good, health and fertile situation; the freehold of which shall remain the property of the Commonwealth; the ground only to be let on building or other leases, all buildings to be erected under strict Government regulations, with due regard to public health and architectural beauty.]

It had been a burning question in the New south Wales well before federation that the site of a national capital be situated in the State not closer than 100 miles from Sydney, and the New South Wales Government lost no time in seeking suitable spot to offer federal government. Individual and organisations responded to an official invitation submitted the locations from Eden in the south, Hay in the west and as far north as Tenterfield..Alexander Oliver, president of the Lands Appeals Court was then commissioned in November 1899 to investigate the sites and make a recommendation tot the New South Wales Government. Oliver rejected all of the sites not on the railway line from Sydney to Burke, stating the site be fairly accessible by the ordinary lines of communication to the most densely peopled part of the constituted States. He had examined twenty there other suggestions, held enquire at fourteen and conclude that the land area of 100 miles was not nearly enough for a federal territory. He finally recommended the first choice be 1200 square miles at Bombala with access to the port of Eden and Orange. The Sydney Bulletin showed interest in the site and editor James Edmund came to the belief that the federal territory should be at least 5000 square miles in area and urged a site of high elevation with all land held by the Crown.

 Barton, as first Prime Minister, wrote to Lee, the premier of New south wales on 13th April 1901, asking if the State were prepared to offer sites. Lee responded by sending Olivers report and offered one of three recommended sites. So that was the situation when O' Malley, who had always showed a keen interest in land acquisition, rose on 19th July to move his motion. It took another eight years of debating and legal wrangling before in 1909 New South Wales transferred the land for the creation of the Federal Capital Territory to federal control through two pieces of legislation, the Seat of Government Acceptance Act 1909 and the Seat of Government Surrender Act 1909. So it was then that the Federal Government began to acquire land and it remained in accord with the legislation enacted in 1910. O' Malley, through all the debating in Parliament and the legal delays in legislation had given his opinion in the years before the reality of the land acquisition for the site and the building of national capital. When Austin Chapman, the member for Eden- said that all members felt the capital should be established as soon as possible, O'Malley interrupted to say 'we shall not be there within ten years' and " We do not want to live in a woodshed."

It was also O' Malley's influence over the fresh faced young genius architect Burly Griffin, a recent arrival from America, to enter the competition to design the new capital. Labor's victory in both houses at the 1910 election again brought Fisher to office, and, this time, O'Malley was elected by caucus and appointed Minister for Home Affairs. He had very strong views on the role of the minister and soon found himself in conflict with his senior officers, especially Colonel David Miller and others whom he termed 'gilt-spurred roosters'. Responsible for the planning of the new national capital, he threw himself into the task with enthusiasm, although previously he had been heard to say that the Federal government should remain in Melbourne and that the site selected was 'a howling wilderness'. Controversy over the design of the new city was resolved when O'Malley endorsed the view of a majority of the selection committee, approving the plan of fellow-American Walter Burley Griffin. Through all his troubles in Australia, Griffin had a firm supporter in his friend. O'Malley had hoped that the capital would be named Shakespeare or Myola.' O'Malley's aggressive partitioned parliament to get going on the land acquisition. It was fitting therefore that King O'Malley, as the Home Affairs Minister drove the first peg in the site for Canberra, the national capital in 1913.

O' Malley back in the early debates on the idea of a national capital land acquisition had to bide his time on moving his cherished motion on an old Age pension. It was a critical necessity for him to put forward his motion being mindful of his constituents and the voting for the retention of his seat in the next election. He first moved the idea after the debate had died down somewhat on the proposed site of the National Capital.

"That, in the opinion of this House, it is desirable, in the interest of the deserving aged poor, that the Government should, without unnecessary delay, formulate a national scheme for payment of old age pensions, and that this motion, when carried, be an instruction for the Attorney general to draft the necessary measure."

Tasmania was divided into electorates for the second Federal election in 1903 when O'Malley narrowly won Darwin. When the short-lived Watson government was formed in 1904, he hoped for a ministerial post but was not considered. Following the defeat of Labor, Prime Minister Sir George Reid was pressured by both the Liberal and Labor parties to inquire into the possibility of establishing old-age pensions. In recognition of his interest, O'Malley was appointed a member of the select committee (1904) and of the subsequent royal commission (1905-06) on the subject. On 10th June 1908 the newly formed Commonwealth Parliament passed the Invalid and Old-Age Pensions Act. The legislation was groundbreaking. Prior to that, the elderly or infirm received no financial support and their care fell either to family, religious and charitable institutions, or government asylums.

While O' Malley's part in the foundation of Canberra and in the building of the transcontinental railway are important events in the modern history of Australia, those Australians who remembered him in after years, probably would agree that his most important and controversial role was that which he played in the foundation of the Commonwealth Bank.

CHAPTER 7.

FRUSTRATED PERFORMER

O'Malley's manner of presenting an argument and his devout devil-may-care attitude, unsubstantiated opinions and frequent interruptions of opponents in the midst of their presenting a motion infuriated them within and outside the House of Parliament and he attracted enemies. Yet, even his enemies in government acknowledged his knowledge of banking and finance and his interest in these subjects. It was obvious that the few years he spent in his uncle's bank in New York in his youth, he had acquired a basic understanding of banking practices and banking needs which was far beyond that of almost all his contemporaries in both in his time in State and Federal Parliaments.

As far back as first setting foot on Australian soil, O'Malley had been interested in the cause of banking reform. He was far from being the first in Australia to advocate banking reform and establishment of State owned banks, for as far back as the middle years of the nineteenth century the issue had been prominent, and considered urgent as a result of the appalling distress caused by massive banking failures of the early 1890s.

W.A. Holmes support of O' Malley's idea of a national banking system was to prove of crucial importance to getting his demands put on the 1908 Labor Conference fighting platform agenda. For it was clearly evident the selection committee on the issue had historically contradictory views on national savings in a capitalist economy and they lacked precision on the ideas. Although the first Commonwealth Government knew that its main concern had to be with the machinery measures and with tariff, it very soon did show that it understood the importance of banking reform. It was O'Malleys persistence in raising the issue of a national bank and his efforts to educate his fellow members and the public at large in the first ten years of Commonwealth Parliament that his driving force sowed the seed to see the Commonwealth Bank become a reality.

Although deeply concerned with social issues, from 1905 O'Malley's dominant interest was banking. As a Tasmanian delegate to the Commonwealth Political Labor Conference in July he sought unsuccessfully to include a proposal for a state bank of deposit and issue in the party's fighting platform; a national bank was, however, placed on the general platform. After paying tribute to M. Cuplin, the member for Brisbane, who had put forward the idea of a Commonwealth currency, O' Malley proposed a state bank of issue which would enjoy the powers that processed by a monopoly of a few private banks. If the state had the control of issue of paper money it could increase notes in circulation in boom times and decrease supply in times of economic necessity. The Treasure Forrest was unresponsive and the House members were apathetic, and it took a year later before O' Malley again had a chance to speak in parliament on banking. Explaining in more detail his idea of a Commonwealth national postal banking system, he was at pains to point out that Labor party was not responsible for his remarks and that : King O' Malley is the architect of his own superstructure. I consult no one as to what I should say... If the Commonwealth had a bank of issue and discount, under the management of a Comptroller-General, who would be entitled to be removed from political control, paper money could be issued for the payment of salaries and for liquidation of other debts incurred by the Commonwealth. The commonwealth notes could be made a legal tender.

In 1907 the Melbourne Punch, whilst often wide of the mark with their belief of O' Malley principles, wrote a portrait of the man that was the usual in conservative circles.

[King O' Malley, though he is now an older Parliamentary hand, still represents the more eccentric development in Australian democracy... From nationhood to party politics, the basis principles in dealing is 'What is there in it for O' Malley? '... the impenetrable brashness with which he faces contumely, ridicule and exposure; his ingenuous pretence of bustle; all things are so much advertisement by which this weird graft Western American extravagance upon Australian socialism hopes to advance his own interest. With him democracy is a business to be exploited as conscientiously as life insurance canvassing. The Black- headed Eagle of the Rocky Mountains has adopted a simple and effective plan of getting on in politics-the plan of notoriety. Anything on earth will do for him, so long as it serves the purpose of getting him talked about. Pressing his hip-pocket, and as likely as not you will find a pistol hiding there for his whole pose is theatrically' Western'...

The eloquent harangues which he delivered against the wicked people who amass money endeared him to the miners who have poured into the sleepy island...

For a time his weird antics were noticed by the newspapers, as some relief from the majestic dullness with which the first Commonwealth Parliament wasa at first treated...By and by the newspapers tired of reporting him and no mater what he said, nobody printed it. Mr. O' Malley is no fool. The matter that is in his vein was exhausted and he relapsed into comparative silence...

But O' Malley on the platform is glob and effective. It is not to educate audiences that he wants to make his appeal, and his rough, course humour, his unexpected quips of phrase and invective 'go down' like fresh oysters with a crowd of miners and navvies'.

He has the faculty, which many well-informed speakers lack, of measuring such an audience, and getting a grip on its flavour. the constituents who elect him are not hungry for political philosophy and nice balance judgement. They want something hot and ranking flavoured...O' Malley gives them a feast of reeking Frankfurt sau usage and peppered sauce, and nice balance judgement., and their plates appreciated it...

No member of the Federal Parliament has been keener than King O' Malley to have the 'screw' raise from 400 pounds to 600 pounds a year. He, at any rate, has been urging it openly, with an audacity in keeping with his methods. While the Senate was discussing the measure, he could not remain in the House, but sat in the gallery listening with strained attention to every word that was spoken. When it was evident that the Senate was going too agree to the grab, the look of joyous relief on his face was comical...

 Some day, doubtless, the miners will grow weary of King O' Malley and he will leave Parliament...Whatever may happen, O' Malley is too skilful in achieving notoriety to be altogether submerged.]

Whilst Parliament opened on 20th February1907, the real opening was delayed until 3rd July for Deakin's return from the Prime Ministers conference in London. The GG outlined a programme of proposed legislations of which there were five that put a smile on the dial of O' Malley. He was not interested in the prospects of legislation to encourage manufacturing or in the increased allocation for defence but he was certainly interested in the prospectus to introduce federal age pensions , to allow the States to tax federal salaries and allowances, to allow for preferential voting for the Parliament, to introduce an insurance and measures to control bills of exchange, cheques, and promissory notes and to establish uniform company and bankruptcy laws.

Before any of these proposals were introduced, members of the House took part in an adjournment debate on patent medications and this gave O' Malley an opportunity to put forward a proposal which was still being vigorously debated nearly seven years later. On 24th July 1907 O' Malley declared: I agree with the honourable member for White Bay (Fisher) that there are thousands of honest and sincere people who require medical attention and medicine, but who are not in a financial position to pay the fees. Under these circumstances, this great and powerful Commonwealth ought to set aside a certain amount annually in order to pay medical men for looking after the poor of the country. I go further, and would have the State pay all doctors; and I would have them put on the same plane as in China- they should cure the patient or have their head cut off. So the idea of a pharmaceutical benefits scheme and Bulk-billing for doctors fees could well be attributed as being the brainchild of King O' Malley.

Apart from the idea of free scripts and bulk billing by doctors, O' Malley always had the proposal of an age pensions scheme and was justly please with the bill being before the house, he also took opportunities to introduce his idea of a national bank which often come to the forefront in his motions to the house.

"The financing of a Commonwealth old age pension scheme would be very simple, with a national postal banking system operated by Australians for the benefit of Australia, utilising the collective power of the Commonwealth and acting as a clearing house for the people of Australia. With such a bank controlling the interest of the Commonwealth, States and Municipalities, we could not only finance old-age pensions, but successfully manage the business in connection with the public indebtedness. But we have never had the courage to tackle this question of instituting a national bank."

In 1908 O'Malley presented to parliament a detailed plan for the creation of a national bank of deposit, issue, exchange and reserve, and in the same year at the third Federal conference of the A.L.P. succeeded in transferring creation of a 'Commonwealth Bank' to the fighting platform. Despite this, O'Malley knew that many party members were lukewarm and he devoted the next two years to educating them. Partly because of his bad relations with Prime Minister Fisher and William Morris Hughes, O'Malley was not elected by caucus to the ministry in 1908. His long standing interruptions of Hughes in his motions to the House only brought an increased personal dislike to this " American bounder' in the eyes of the man. It may be hearsay, but a story which does not appear in parliamentary Hansards abounds that Hughes on one occasion kept calling out over O' Malley: I want to pass a motion, I want to pass a motion."

Where upon O' Malley quipped: "I suggest then that you pass it in the House in preference to taking its stench home to your family. Likewise the privy is that way, so I further suggest you take all your papers that you hold before you, for I feel sure you will need the lot of it."

Fisher and Hughes were not convinced of the need for a national bank before the government was defeated in June 1909. But party support was growing for a competing bank which would smash the 'Money Power'. Banking had long been one of King O'Malley's keenest interests as a politician. In 1905 he unsuccessfully advanced a proposal for a state-owned bank of deposit and issue to become part of Labor's campaign platform. In 1908, he presented a detailed plan to parliament for the creation of a government owned bank of deposit, issue, exchange and reserve. In pursing these policies, he often met with significant resistance from senior party figures such as William Morris 'Billy' Hughes and Andrew Fisher, who were not persuaded of its immediate necessity. Moreover, Fisher and Hughes favoured a bank that would be commercial in nature and provide competition to the private banks as a repository for savings. The Fisher Government lost office in 1909, before a bank of any kind could be established.

Fisher returned as Prime Minister at the 1910 election and O'Malley was appointed Minister for Home Affairs. O'Malley's lobbying efforts, supported by a 'torpedo brigade' of 19 supporters in the Labor caucus bore fruit in 1911, with the government legislating to establish a national bank. However, the form of the new Commonwealth Bank was not what O'Malley had envisaged with central banking responsibilities, with the power to issue money and finance government debt. Nor was it to act as a source of cheap credit for farmers and small businesses. Instead, the new government owned bank was to be operated on a commercial basis, similar to the privately owned banks already operating in Australia. This was a source of bitter disappointment to O'Malley, for it was not his idea of a Commonwealth Bank. As established, it was, without doubt, a Fisher bank, but it may be claimed that O'Malley was the spiritual father of the later Commonwealth and Reserve banks. The Commonwealth Bank adopted more of the functions and responsibilities of a central bank. In 1924, it became fully responsible for the issue of banknotes. In 1945, the *Commonwealth Bank Act 1945* and *Banking Act 1945* were passed, giving a legislative basis to various central banking roles and functions that the Commonwealth Bank had assumed over previous decades, particularly during WW11. In undergoing these changes, the Bank began to more closely resemble the institution O'Malley had advocated for.

In his later years, he was known to pay visits to the Commonwealth Bank's Melbourne branch and distribute business cards describing himself as the 'Founder of the Commonwealth Bank' and published a wide range of literature promoting himself as such. It would be inaccurate to describe O'Malley as the Bank's founder. That this role has at times been attributed to him is partly a reflection at his own talent for self-promotion within his lifetime. The push to create a 'national bank' preceded his arrival in Australia by many years and involved a number of significant public figures. Moreover, the institution created in 1911 was one created in a form much more of Andrew Fisher's preference than of O'Malley's. It is, however, fair to credit him with the increased public consciousness of the issue and for rallying support within the governing Labor Party. O'Malley effectively seized important opportunities and his efforts and initiative contributed substantially to the foundation of the institution that later evolved into the Reserve Bank we know today. He produced a booklet in his retirement years entitled 'The Commonwealth Bank- The Facts of its Creation'- a self promotional detail of his pioneering the bank from its time of foundation.

The O' Malley claim to be founder of Australia's national banking system was all of O'Malleys projects of self promoting. He had an insatiable desire to be liked and had the frustration of attempting to cement his positions views and news into a reality so that he might be remembered more than a headstone on a grave. It is the way with those who have been saddled with the slings and arrows of abandonment in childhood.

On 10 May 1910 in Melbourne, giving his age as 51 and describing himself as a widower since 1886, O'Malley had married Amy Garrod, a New Zealander; they had no children. He had property in Seattle, Oregon, and invested in many more houses in Melbourne, some of them slum cottages. A consistent supporter of the rights of women, O'Malley immediately on his marriage ensured that his wife was financially independent. Tall and still bearded, with his flowing tawny hair, O'Malley had an arresting and, to many, an irritating presence. His mocking, mischievous personality contributed to the controversy he deliberately invited, but his verbal clowning never entirely obscured the complex and hard-headed man who was perhaps 'his own worst enemy'.

Labor lost office in 1913 but O'Malley easily retained his seat then, and in 1914 when Fisher again became Prime Minister. However, in view of the hostility of Fisher, Hughes and Pearce, he was not elected to the ministry. The outbreak of WW I placed O'Malley, a convinced pacifist representing a strongly patriotic constituency, in an uncomfortable position. His growing hostility to Australia's part in the war distanced him even further from the party leaders and he moved closer to the radical anti-war faction. Following Fisher's resignation in 1915, O'Malley was elected to the Hughes ministry, again as Home Affairs Minister, where he found himself under constant attack from his Labor predecessor W.O. Archibald. The construction of Canberra proceeded slowly and a series of scandals over the building of the transcontinental railway gave ammunition to his enemies. His idiosyncratic dealings with his departmental staff became increasingly difficult and he was unable to command their loyalty.

During 1916, while not active as an anti-conscription advocate, O'-Malley refused to resign his portfolio despite Hughes's pressure. He finally lost office on 13th November when Hughes and twenty-four other members left caucus to form the National Labor ministry. In the 1917 election O'Malley was defeated decisively in his pro-conscription electorate. He was defeated again for Denison in 1919 and for Bass in 1922 when he stood as an independent Labor candidate.
Although he was only 63 at the time of his defeat, he retired in Melbourne devoting his time to building up his legacy. In retirement he constantly asserted his claim to be the true founder of the Commonwealth Bank, promulgating varying versions of his role. Two of his close friends, Dorothy Catts in her *King O'Malley Man and Statesman* (Sydney, 1957) and L. C. Jauncey in his *Australia's Government Bank* (London, 1933), faithfully backed his claims.

CHAPTER 8.

THE LAST HURRAH

There is a vital difference between the position of Ministers under Liberal government rules as opposed to rules of appointment under Labour. Liberal ministers, being selected by the favour of the Prime Minister, can only hold office during his pleasure and must resign should they disagree with the policy or methods of their leader. Labour Ministers, on the other hand, are selected by a vote of the whole Party and derive their authority from that source, consequently only that authority which elects possess the power of withdrawal. The personal policy of the Prime Minister does not necessarily determine the attitude of other Ministers, for the Prime Minister is himself amenable to the same authority and has no personal prerogative from his position as elected leader of the Party.

It must be recognised that no individual person can know everything. No man possesses all the virtues, and as always no individual in political history is infallible, except maybe the exception to the rule is Jesus of Nazareth and mankind crucified him. No question, local, national nor international is settled until it is rightfully and righteously settled. Any other disposition or inherent qualities of mind or character is only temporary. Intellectual brilliance, like much of O' Malley's sometime focus utterances, but exercise without scruple and sound judgement were found to be a power wandering in a jungle.

But it was not just O' Malley whose powers of persuasion failed him in politics in the long run, for his own party may well have let him down to when reign ended in disarray. For history attested to the failure of so many brilliant Ministers,; great men like Honoré Gabriel Riqueti, Count of Mirabeau who was a French writer, orator, statesman and a prominent figure of the early stages of the French Revolution. A member of the nobility, Mirabeau had been involved in numerous scandals that had left his reputation in ruins. Another by way of example was Sir Francis Bacon, lord chancellor of England (1618–21). A lawyer, statesman, philosopher, and master of the English tongue, is remembered in literary terms for the sharp worldly wisdom of a few dozen essays; by students of constitutional history or his power as a speaker in Parliament and in famous trials and intellectually as a man who claimed all knowledge as his province and, after a magisterial survey, urgently advocated new ways by which man might establish a legitimate command over nature for the relief of his estate. In 1593 he took a stand objecting to the government's intensified demand for subsidies to help meet the expenses of the war against Spain. The queen (Elizabeth 1) took offence, and Bacon was in disgrace during several critical years when there were chances for legal advancement.

Then there are those like career disgraced men- plodders like writer John Bunyan who was jailed for his spiritual beliefs but life taught him too face suffering with gratitude and he became famous as a novelist. Bunyan's best work being Pilgrims Progress. Likewise Abe Lincoln after many failures in life and business as a lawyer became the United States' 16th President in 1861. Iissuing the Emancipation Proclamation that declared forever free those slaves within the Confederacy in 1863, but in the fall of Richmond on April 3, 1865, and Lee's surrender at Appomattox on April 9, there were southern sympathisers who believed the Confederacy could be restored.. John Wilkes Booth held that belief, and it was the motive behind his plot to murder President Abraham Lincoln.

The press were relentless when it come to O' Malley's in house sole views in debating a cause [It must be remembered that the Australian labour cause is not a one man movement. One leader may die, another may get tired , and still another desert to the enemy, but the soul of Australian Labour marches on. The movement started back with half starved, hard pressed, leg ironed convicts and fought its way to robust manhood and its cause will continue in orderly advance to the goal whence its sceptre will result over a cooperative Commonwealth., abounding in the blessings, and benefits which flow from just and righteous laws, under which privileged class is entrenched but which secures free and equal opportunity for all citizens. The Argus Melbourne, 14th November 1916.]

The Caucus met in a special meeting on the 15th November 1916 and sixty four members were present. As soon the minutes of the previous meeting had been confirmed, Finalson moved 'That Mr W.M. Hughes no longer possesses the confidence of the party as leader and that the office of chairman of this party be, and is hereby declared vacant. After a lengthy debate, which lasted well into the afternoon, Hughes suddenly left the chair and, calling those who supported him to follow, left the room. Some twenty-four party members including close acquaintances of O' Malley, being Bamford, Chanter, Spencer, de Largie and Webster up and left too. Later that evening O' Malley and Mahon tendered their resignation. It was not an easy decision for O' Malley to steel himself to resign the ministry and revert to a role on the opposition backbench, despite the fact that his rooted loyalty was still with Labour. In his diary notes of 14th December he entered 'determined to resist all Billy's mongrelism'.

So to recap on the political life of this character who first sat as an independent before joining the Australian Labor Party, representing mining and pastoral communities in Western Tasmania. Despite being a popular and prominent Labor figure, O'Malley was something of a maverick within his party. This was due to his atypical background and flamboyant style andalso his political positions, which were often more radical than those of his caucus colleagues. It was at O'Malley's suggestion that the party revised the spelling of its name to the American style, 'Labor', which he argued would present a more modern image. O'Malley was passed over for ministerial service in the short-lived Reid Labor Government, however with the election of the Fisher Labor Government, O'Malley served as Minister for Home Affairs from 1910 to 1913.

He was reappointed to this ministry in the Hughes Government between 1915 and 1916. These appointments saw him involved in projects of national significance, such as the construction of Australia's transcontinental railway. There was much controversy over O'Malley's appointment of Henry Chinn, an unproven and unqualified person as Chief Engineer of the railway construction and as the cost of construction blew out it giving the opposition party and some members of labor to argue the case against the appointment and questioned O'Malley in his capacity as Home Affairs Minister in his approval of the Chinn' appointment without consulting the House of Parliament. Like all things O' Malley, he was flamboyant in his right as the decision maker and managed to get enough backing to justify his decision. Likewise for the identification of Canberra as the site of Australia's capital city and the selection of architect Walter Burley Griffin's design for it. O'Malley proved himself to be an important ally and enthusiastic supporter of Griffin in the building and construction of the capital, whose work was otherwise stymied by bureaucratic and political resistance, had Griffin been taken off the job.

So we draw the curtain on O' Malley's 1916 political year for unbeknown to him at the time a turning point to his future life was on the horizon. The year had begun with O' Malley still holding the post as Minister for Home Affairs and it appeared back then that he had the command of his department. He had reinstated Griffin and hoped for the rapid development for the federal capital; as he had done and achieved with the transcontinental railway would progress smoothy to completion. The Commonwealth Bank idea was growing with strength and influence and the echoes of 'the Chinn affair' had died down, and he could well expect to see, as Minister, the the period until the next election in 1917. However by the end of the year most of his high hopes had turned to ashes. It was obvious to all that things in Home Affairs was not to the liking of the ranks and file under O' Malley's leadership. His dealings with his officers proved that he could no longer command their loyalty.

The progress in work of Canberra had proceeded slowly and painfully amid construction reports of waste and industrial unrest. The Chinn affair had been resurrected and his appointment by O' Malley's subordinate Gilchrist had proved too naive. O' Malley in question time had to make a humiliating climb down the face of union pressure. Finally not only was he no longer a minister but the Labor Party, to whose service he had devoted much of his life, were in disarray and unlikely to occupy the Treasury benches for a very long time. Even for such an ebullient spirit as O' Malley it had been a very depressing twelve months.

The First World War placed O'Malley in an awkward political position. Whilst he was himself a committed pacifist, the constituency he represented was strongly in favour of Australia's involvement in the war. His anti-war and anti-conscription stance contributed to his alienation from cabinet and his defeat at the 1917 election. It was the first time in his life that O' Malley was without a job and he found the days grandly slow between sun up and sundown. Initially he had little to do but contemplate and was some what melancholy. He filled in his days at the race track, supervising renovations of his slum dwellings and visiting his tenants. The press lost interest for a time in O'Malley except a reporter at the time hoping for a story began to call on tenants to see what kind of landlord King had become. No tenants had anything but deep respect for O' Malley and found him to be a kind and fair man in the level of rent he charged them. One Chinese tenant had remarked: *"King O'Malley, he a fair man, him goof fellow, he tell me joke about Chinese chicken."*

For one being used too much vigorous activity it was an unsatisfactory life for him. He had always wanted to leave a mark of his time on earth instead of being remembered only by a headstone. He had to reached that age of understanding that we should live in this life but not of it. Still he soon found himself back on the campaign trail with the view of rebuilding his political base.

At the dawn of 1918 the Labor Party, led by Frank Tudor, was still in disarray, but hope was returning and O'Malley found his despondency lift from his former defeat, and he began to look around for a seat for which he might nominate in the pending Federal election due in November or December 1919. He realised that he was unlikely to win Darwin, or indeed Tasmania. So he set his sites on South Australia, the only state where he still had the political clout and helpful connections. He began his campaigns early as March 1918 in Adelaide, feeling out the situation and speaking to labor groups at every opportunity. It was far too early to get any preselection and for most of the years he had to content himself at home, making visits to the race track and receiving visits from Labor party friends who were still at in Federal Parliament.

King O' Malley had not been touched much by the war but he knew well that his staunch conscientious objection to sending our troops to fight in Europe between 1914 to war end meant that he would find it difficult to get preselection. Back in Adelaide again in 1919 he tramped the streets seeking help all who could back him. He was back dressed to the nines in his outlandish style- big tie with opal pin under his greying beard, trench coat over three piece suit- and with his American accent still untouched by over thirty years residency in Australia. He was no-doubt an impressive figure who found himself far removed form the novice members for Encounter Bay. But those who have memories like elephants, particularly the likes of a conservative electorate of which he hoped to get support forhis campaign for preselection were not impressed any more by the rhetorical theatrical style of the King. Likewise in Adelaide memoir of O' Malley's anti-war stance, the railway fiasco with The Chinn Affair and multiple other minor wrongdoings did not fare well for him. So King returned to Melbourne once again and by the end of June he knew he had to look elsewhere.

Like any man of an inflatable ego when the balloon is busted psychoso-
matic illness returns, but soon the lumbago passed as soon as he was elected as delegate to the Interstate labor Conference in Sydney in October. By
this time he had decided to stand again for the Tasmanian electorate of
Denison while his friend Joseph Lyon, later to be Prime Minister, stood for
Darwin. In the local electorate for labor preselection on November 10th he
easily defeated his rival return soldier and continued his campaign with
-out being endorsed for the party seat. King O'Malley was back at his
oratory best with large attendance at his public speeches, but the press ignored his meetings and focused, their attention on the Nationalist opponent, Laird Smith who had left the labour Party with Hughes. By the time
the elections came around in December the war had been over for more
than a year. But the passions aroused over conscription had not abated and
O'Malley deprived of much publicity by then actions of the Mercury had
left him knowing that the would have a hard fight to win the seat.

When the counting was complete the Nationalist had a victory over Labor.
O'Malley had polled well and was certainly not disgraced, but it was apparent to all but himself that his days of catching votes in Tasmania were
over, and at the age of 61 he was finished as a politician. It was then he
withdrew from public life. So he returned once more to domestic affairs
and his life with wife Amy, but he found life increasingly empty. He often
walked to and from the city and entertained politician friends of the past
and Griffin, a subordinate architect of Walter Burley Griffith to whom he
began to see a great deal.

In 1919 Griffin had began the search for a site on Sydney Harbour suitable
for comprehensive development and eventually secured an option to purchase 263 hectares (650 acres) of land with 6.44 kilometres (4 miles) of
water frontage which included large portions of the areas now known as
Castle-crag, Castle Cove and Middle Cove. It was then he formed a company, the Greater Sydney Development Association (GSDA), to purchase
and develop the estate. It was to be a model of how to subdivide, develop
and build within, and with respect for, the Australian landscape.
 Griffin had been the moving spirit in the negotiations for the land and in
the company articles nobody except him could hold 'A' class shares and
he was named Managing Director. Griffin had been enchanted by Sydney
Harbour and its foreshores ever since he arrived by ship from Chicago
USA in 1913 to take up the position of Federal Capital Director of Design

and Construction after winning the Canberra competition the previous year. When Griffin resigned from this position in 1920, he and his architect wife Marion Griffin poured their vast energies into establishing a residential development that was sympathetic to this beautiful natural environment, unlike the red roofs and grid streets that characterised Sydney at the time.

 Griffin had considerable experience in estate planning and development in the United States and he continued his town planning activity after arriving in Australia. He planned a number of estates around Melbourne as well as town centres for Griffith in the Murrumbidgee Irrigation Area of NSW and schemes for Port Stephens and Jervis Bay. Griffin believed that better suburban environments could be created by careful planning that respected the landscape character of an area itself together with the provision of community open spaces within an increased number of allotments. These theories were to be tested and proven in his work at Castlecrag.

The formation of the GSDA involved a number of shareholders of diverse backgrounds who supported the Griffins and their ideals and who had appointed Griffin as Managing Director. It was more run like a co-operative in its operation with forty five 1000 pound shares holders, including among them Griffin, O' Malley, Agar Wynn, a lawyer who began his career in the Victorian Legislative Council and served two terms as Solicitor-General of Victoria and later in the House of Representatives, and James Catts, politician and unionist, Sir Elliott Johnson, a long-serving member of the House of Representatives, and Sir Austin Chapman who also served in the House of Representatives during O' Malley's term as Minister for Home Affairs. Griffin chose the name 'Castlecrag', having been inspired by Edinburgh Rock — a sandstone outcrop forming the highest point within the rocky peninsula projecting into Middle Harbour. Shareholders of GSDA were offered a free block of land if they built a house upon it and the resulting 'demonstration houses' were constructed in 1921 and 1922, the first years of the estate.

Strangely for a successful architect Griffin was always short of money and would have been in considerable difficulty if it had not been for bank guarantees by O' Malley and other friends. The company had a chequered history before it was wound up in the 1940s when promise of large profits were deferred. Shareholders grew tired of profit delay and were not liking the houses designed by Griffith, in addition, the banks would not back the project. Things turned from bad to worst forcing O' Malley and the majority of shareholders to go to the Equity Court in an attempt to force Griffin out. Despite this the two men remained friends even though O' Malley no longer admired his friend abilities especially in matters of money and for that matter architectural knowledge.

By 1922 O' Malley had become bored and restless. He was still a fit active 63 year old, and none the less needed a mission to pursue. Wife Amy had been recovering from a dangerous illness and once he saw that she was well enough, he determined he would try one more attempt at Federal Parliament. So on the 31st May he arrived in Launceston to kindly patronage of Labor preselection-his time for the seat of Bass. Being the extraverted man of Irish charm he turned on the charm to win over the party members. But once again his efforts were in vain and by October he learnt the party had chosen another candidate. Undeterred he declared his intention to stand as an independent labor candidate an at once launched an all out campaign.

His audiences were treated with the whole story of his Australian parliamentary life from his overseeing of the building of the Trans-Continental railway, to the securing of land and the Building of Canberra, and his part as founder of the Commonwealth bank. He took self praise for this at the time of his position a step Minister fro Home Affairs. They heard how he had tried to secure the land for the building of the Sydney G.P.O. and in 1911 had prepared a bill to provide unemployment insurance and general life insurance and had only failed because cabinet had 'knocked him out'. With appetites full this recital of his achievements and near misses, his listeners were undoubtedly happier with his launch on the description of the Prime Minister than his former-rant on the great King O' Malley.

In no way did the great King consider it necessary to say what he might do for the constituents in Bass but felt that his political history was enough to win him additional votes had them within gadded attack on the Prime Minister. Brother Hughes, the Prime Minister, is neither loved nor hated his his colleagues. He is affable, courteous, a hale fellow well met with the rank and file of all parties. He is without convictions or seep prejudices on may subject. No one is much concerned as to his want or constructive ability or original political ideas...No promise was or is too wild or fantastic for him to make. No controversy was too keen *for him to side-step or acquiesce in it. No issue so sharply drawn but that he could accept either side or both at the same meeting...*

But audiences in Bass in 1922 were apathetic, even to the famous O' Malley brand of crowd oratory, and it was apparent to him, long before the poll, that he had little chance of winning the seat. What must have depressed him however, was the small number of votes he actually received. No longer could there be any doubt, even in his eyes, that he was a spent political force. He could have done no worst than sprout the message of temperance and the dangers of his version of alcohol abuse which he called 'stagger juice,' For he may well have scored more votes from the abused wives of alcholics, the still suffering alcholics themselves and the public at large who were mindful of the effects of the alcoholic abuse. It had after all been his prime cause for a lifetime and the paradox is that he was mindful of the precious gift of sobriety and knew how to appeal to the minds of those still suffering alcholics in his oratory as much to the spirit of the sober public on that subject matter.

So finally but reluctantly O'Malley retired, having another thirty two years to live a long to a busy life and one which he found it hard to occupy. He always, at least publicly remained gregarious, and found solace in the long procession of friends and acquaintances, both political and non political, who visited the little house in Bradford Street. Together, like all of the retired populous of any age, there was more to talk about from the past than their remaining years and they too listened remembered the past political fights of the King.

So what remained then was his concern for the future of 'his' Commonwealth Bank, and became his main issue for the remainder of his years as he followed its ups and downs, seeking always to pursue those in power-be they of the national lists, Labor or Country Party- to turn the vision of his 1908 banking and finance ideas into reality. When (Sir) Earl Page became Treasure in 1923 he quickly earned the Kings approval-despite being the leader of the Country Party when he introduced banking legislation in accordance with the King O' Malley blue print. He remained a close friend for the rest of his O'Malleys life, being a frequent visitor to the house in Albert park. Page was convinced that: [...the history (of the way)... and the close interdependence of State- Commonwealth financial relations demonstrated that, had the Commonwealth Bank been given the status of a central rather than a competitive bank at its inception, the financing of the war would have been greatly simplified.

When the question of the founding for the Commonwealth Bank was raised O' Malley was particularly concerned to have his version of the events of 1911 accepted and to the very end of his life he spread his story by letters, newspaper story, a book on its foundation and by radio. Although he was determined to have himself recognised as the actual founder of the Commonwealth Bank, O' Malley, up to the last ten years, kept clearly in mind the need to strengthen the bank against conservative attack. He was delighted when the Menzies Government was defeated in 1941 and a Labor Government was formed. In November 1941 he wrote to Ben Chiefly, the new treasurer, to suggest that the Government should peg the shares in trading banks, prevent them issuing any more shares, and make them branches of the commonwealth bank and compensate shareholders by paying them reasonable dividends. Early in 1945 he wrote to Prime Minister Curtin opposing Chiefly's idea of one man control of the bank and suggesting a small board of control. Still concerned about threats to his beloved bank he suggested:

.. if you cannot think of anything better, I would suggest that you put in a law that before any man could close or change or interfere with the business operations of the Commonwealth bank, as a Bank of bankers or general bank, that he must take a Referendum the people...

In the last decade of his life O' Malley constantly referred to himself as a 'death dodger', and became increasingly pre-occupied with what would happen to his estate. He explored various schemes with his lawyers an finally decided in consultation with wife Amy to leave a large portion to accumulate in the King and Amy O'Malley Trust Fund to provide for twenty one years after the death of the last survivor for annual scholarships for girls at a domestic economy. This decision was perhaps the final paradox of his life, from it is clear that. despite having many female friends and a close relationship with his wife, and the efforts that he had made for the rights of women whilst in parliament, he did not particularly like women and was never rarely emotionally or intellectually close to them. Amy was no doubt appalled and objected when he had wanted to call the trust fund 'The King and Rosy O'Malley trust funds.' She ultimately persuaded him to change it to include her name in lieu of a a wife who had died of TB decades before or in truth may never have ever existed.

In the last few years of his life and especially after William Morris Hughes died in 1952, O' Malley the last survivor of the first federal Parliament, once more became a celebrity, and was introduced by the media to a new generation which knew little of the struggles of the first turbulent decade of the century. Frequently interviewed, he had his picture painted as an entry for the Archibald prize and was a 'Guest of Honour' on the SBC radio programme. He was asked to record his speech which he made at the foundation of Canberra in 1912 and his correspondence grew as many old friends wrote to him recalling the past and people unknown to him wrote for his advise on matters from banking to cures for tuberculosis.

In 1952 and 1953 he had two accidents and his eyesight was affected, but his general health was good for a man in his mid nineties, and he had hopes of reaching the century. December 1953 was however a very hot month and quite suddenly on the 20th, while sitting in his bedroom reading a newspaper, he collapsed and died. The Christmas message would have usually been the main news and the Queen's imminent visit, but the widely reported news by the Federal Government of O' Malley's death was to take precedence. For it was reported that O' Malley was to be given a State funeral in St. Paul's Cathedral. The Dean of Melbourne, Dr. Barton Babbage, pointed out that he clearly retained some of the puritanism which had been brought to the United States by the Pilgrim Fathers: **'Later King O' Malley'** he said, **' was a great Australian patriot, one of the most colourful and dynamic figures in the history of our century, a man universally acknowledged for integrity of character.'**

King O' Malley the last survivor of the first Commonwealth parliament, died in his Albert Park home, and was cremated after a state funeral. His estate of over £70,000 and that of his wife who died in 1956 were invested to provide scholarships, eventually thirty a year, for girls in home economics. A portrait of O' Malley by Dudley Drew is still held by the Commonwealth Bank, Melbourne.

The Commonwealth Bank was a Government owned enterprise until the conversion of the Bank into a public company with share capital on 17th April 1991. The stock over the past 32 years has gained a whopping 1887.96% since its initial public offering. In keeping with O' Malley's wishes the stock continues to pay a reasonable dividend return to the shareholders.

The passage of the Reserve Bank Act 1959 resulted in the separation of the Reserve bank from the Commonwealth Bank, to create a stand alone central bank in Australia. After his death in 1953, it was decided by the trustees of O' Malley's estate that the Reserve Bank would be the home for a number of his personal effects, which have been cared for by the bank's archives since their transfer to it in 1964.

CHAPTER 9.

THE EPILOGUE

So in the final analysis of this story let us take a moment to recap this story of King O'Malley life. For some readers may well turn to this page before reading the whole book with the view, like the teller of this tale, to begin within the end in mind. I make no excuse for ignoring less of Hansards or detailed accounts of legislation introduce in Parliament which may be of interest to historians or for that matter bankers and financiers. That was not my intent in writing this story as I alluded to from the the very beginning. It is an account based on as much fiction as fact with a splash of press comments and O' Malley's public speeches, parliament outbursts and funny comments to liven up the plot a tad. If the reader would care to dig a little deeper on this larger than life character of Australian history, I recommend you refer to the reference material described introductory pages.

O' Malley was the grand legend of Australian political history- not so much for his eccentric buffoonery but for his strength of character and dogged determination in seeing through the motions he presented to the House of Parliament as the longest-serving minister to the very end. He was a visionary frustrated by many of his ideas being unacceptable in his time. He was a flamboyant self-publicist whose exploits brought him much ridicule. A fanatically Australian foreigner who proposed all things American for the colony in its political infancy. As a socialist with capitalist views on the day's economy, he amassed a fortune through slum property ownership.

O'Malley came to Australia as a young man and was soon successful as a roving super insurance salesman in Tasmania and South Australia. His bombast manner and Irish charm took him into the South Australian parliament, where his weird campaigns for lavatories and cushions for seats for women on railway trains and the Married Women's Protection League won him notoriety. He was not himself an admirer of womenfolk and seem to have limited association with them accepted for political reasons, but never the less was a giant to raising their status in society. Legends and mystery surround his name, his actual date of birth, and are unravelled in this account of his life. He professed that he was born in Canada but lived his youth in America; he insisted he founded the Waterlily Rockbound

Church- of the Redskin Church of the Cayuse Nation, an ardent preacher of the dangers of alcohol of which he called 'stagger juice, he by his own report never ever drank himself but didn't mind entering hotels to canvass life insurance or introduce his political views to drinkers to elicit votes. He sold life insurance and land deals across the wild west of the Americas and, on arrival in Australia as a sick man with TB, lived in a cave in Queensland for two years, being nursed back to health by an Aboriginal. The fact of his earlier life in America and his tell tale manner of his arrival down under is still yet unproven.

He was a born raconteur whose political career, aided by the style of his 'spread eagle' rhetoric, carried him into the first Federal government, where he continued to be characterised by wild proposals, strong reformist policies and fervent industry know-how. He became Minister for Home Affairs and was instrumental in founding the Commonwealth Bank, the transcontinental railway, and establishing Canberra as the Federal government's centre. His many clashes with colleagues and the public service, not forgetting his public oratory and press criticism over the decades of his working life, kept him in the limelight of politics. He outlived his political enemies, press critics and colleagues and proved to be our most colourful and enigmatic of politicians. O'Malley was a charismatic, gregarious and colourful figure. His considerable intellect and his flair as a salesman contributed to his success both in business and in politics. His mischievous sense of humour charmed many.

Perhaps O' Malley's greatest legacy is his importance in developing the national capital and is remembered in Canberra with the suburb of O'Malley being named after him. A pub in Canberra, 'King O' Malley's Irish Pub' in Civic, is also named after him- a tongue-in -cheek reference to his sponsorship of the unpopular alcohol ban in the Australian Capital Territory during Canberra'a early years. But it would be in O' Malley's view that his funding of the Commonwealth Bank was his greatest achievement.

O'Malley was not in any sense of the words a 'conventional politician.' He was a visionary before this time whose sometimes way out ideas were ridiculed within the House of parliament and in the public view. it was justice to him, that he lived long enough to see many of his ideas accepted and he was able to enjoy that particular status given only to living legends.

It has been a trip down memory lane for me in writing this book but all good things inevitably must come to an end. O'Malley's life is not a template for anyone to emulate in modern day society or politically. However, there are some interesting lessons in critiquing his flamboyant behaviour, zest for living as he willed and his egocentricity that would not be tolerated in todays society let alone in the houses of Parliament. It is my belief that he did a lot more good in his life for others, for our nation and for our financial system than any other Australian to this present day, and in that I salute him.

No man is an island entire of itself; every man
is a piece of the continent, a part of the main;
if a clod be washed away by the sea, Europe
is the less, as well as if a promontory were, as
well as any manner of thy friends or of thine
own were; any man's death diminishes me,
because I am involved in mankind.
And therefore never send to know for whom
the bell tolls; it tolls for thee.

- John Dunn

About the Author.

Doug McPhillips, poet, singer, songwriter, author, commenced his journey of discovery over a decade ago after life changing experiences.

The many tracks he has traversed throughout the Northern Hemisphere and down under in New Zealand and Australia has resulted in the facts and fictions of this novel.

Doug has recorded and sings songs interrelated to this work with majestic melody in a true Australian style.

Doug has written several novels, a book of poems, a travel guide and two albums of his songs all inspired by his adventurers.

www.caminoway.com.au

" A journey of the Spirit."

Doug is an adventurer who divides his time between creative pursuits, family and friends, and those who may benefit most from his efforts and experience.

D.McP July 23.